Gaspard Mermillod

Monseigneur Mermillod on the supernatural life

Being conferences delivered in retreat, to the ladies of Lyons

Gaspard Mermillod

Monseigneur Mermillod on the supernatural life
Being conferences delivered in retreat, to the ladies of Lyons

ISBN/EAN: 9783741193293

Manufactured in Europe, USA, Canada, Australia, Japa

Cover: Foto ©Andreas Hilbeck / pixelio.de

Manufactured and distributed by brebook publishing software
(www.brebook.com)

Gaspard Mermillod

Monseigneur Mermillod on the supernatural life

MONSEIGNEUR MERMILLOD

ON THE

SUPERNATURAL LIFE;

BEING

CONFERENCES DELIVERED, IN RETREAT, TO THE LADIES OF LYONS.

TRANSLATED FROM THE FRENCH,

WITH A PREFACE,

By LADY HERBERT.

LONDON:

R. WASHBOURNE, 18 PATERNOSTER ROW.

1874.

Dedication to Mary.

OST Holy Virgin Mary, Mother of
God; thou whom the Church calls
by the sweetest, the tenderest
names; thou who art both a Virgin Immaculate and the Mother of the Redeemer;
thou whom the Saviour has preserved from
original sin; thou who wast born without
stain, who didst live without blemish, and
die without pain; thou Queen of souls; under
thy protection do we place the fruit of our
retreat. Under thy white banner will we
serve the cause of God, of thy Son; we will
be the servants of charity and of virtue.
We have been told to purify, to supernatu-

ralize our life, to fulfil the law of sacrifice, of self-immolation, and of duty; following thy example, we will become generous, courageous, willing to suffer.

O Virgin Mary, amongst the crowd at thy feet there are many hearts who suffer; comfort them, O thou consoler of the afflicted! There are contrite hearts who have wept and mourned, but who have risen up again, strengthened by the Saviour's blood; help and support them. There are pious and devout souls; cheer and elevate them. Succour all Christian souls. Turn thine eyes upon the spouse of Jesus Christ, and upon us who belong to thee. Look upon those who are in distress and suffering; upon sinners; upon the wandering sheep of Christ's Fold; upon all poor heretics. May thy blessing descend upon us, that we may learn so to understand and to sanctify our earthly life, that we may one day enjoy a life in heaven with thee in the glories of eternity. Amen.

PREFACE.

THE " Retreat," of which a translation has been made in the following pages, forms, as it were, the second part of a series of conferences on the end and aim of human life, given on two separate occasions to the ladies of Lyons.

We believe that there never was a time when the impressive words of this holy and illustrious bishop were more needed than the present.

The struggle which formerly was confined to certain places and certain minds, is now going on all over the world. I mean the struggle between God and the devil; between Faith and unbelief; between those who still revere the Word of God, and the entire negation of all divine Revelation.

Religious subjects are now discussed everywhere with a dangerous facility. There is scarcely a daily newspaper which does not devote a leader to some disputed point in faith or morals. The reviews follow in their wake. In every corner of the earth the evil spirit of doubt and scepticism is prowling round our homes, suggesting to one, this religious difficulty; to another, that; flattering the pride of youth by persuading him that there is something new and original in the line of independent thought which he has struck out: that it was all very well for his father and mother to believe so and so, but that these are old-world ideas, unsuited to the present day, and to the present higher range of intellectual culture.

Tell a young man or a young woman of the nineteenth century that the poorest and most illiterate person who really loves and serves God, will have a higher place in heaven than the wisest and cleverest of their heroes (unless they also have a like grace), and the said young man or woman will simply smile upon you a smile of scornful pity for your ignorance and narrow-mindedness. With a presumption, which would make one laugh if one were not more inclined to cry, they discuss the deepest mysteries of the Christian faith at all times and at all seasons. They walk boldly where even angels fear to tread. Everything in the heavens above and in the earth below is treated by them as an open question, to be subjected to the criticism of their unschooled minds, and to be tested in the crucible of their own limited yet conceited apprehension.

One marvels more and more at the patience of God in bearing with this ignorance and folly, when one hears the youth of both sexes thus laying down the law, and inventing a new Christianity for themselves, while they sneer at what they term the narrow-minded prejudices of those who still keep to the old paths of faith and duty. Hence, too, arises contempt of parents; disobedience to authority; and all the evils which follow in their train.

Take again the popular literature of the day. I do not mean the novels, though they are bad enough, but the multitude of clever and interesting works, treating on these very subjects of human reason and faith, literature and dogma, with, I had almost said, a *diabolical* charm. They are written in beautiful language; they are full of admirable descriptions and delicate imagery, and are, in many cases, imbued with a thoroughly poetic and artistic spirit, which makes them specially attractive to cultivated minds. But under these fair flowers the serpent lurks—the serpent of scepticism and unbelief. And the worst of it is, that even with good people, people who would shrink with horror from the idea of denying their faith, the doubts suggested in these books stick and leave a bad impression. Oh! the devil knows what he is about; and the poison spread by him is well and skilfully laid! And although any one conversant with theology could, in a moment, overturn all their apparently beautiful fabric of error, and demonstrate its folly, yet the misfortune is, that to do so requires a deeper and fuller treatment of the subject than suits the taste of such readers: and so the answers to these dangerous books are simply laid aside unread, with, perhaps, the careless or contemptuous reply: "Such works are not in my line."

But Mgr. Mermillod has gone further, and shown

how the tempter, with consummate skill, has actually succeeded in convincing men of his own non-existence, in order the better to work out his nefarious purposes. The devil is now considered, by young men especially, as simply a "humanly invented Bogie"—I am quoting the very words of a well-known writer—meant only to frighten women and children.

Point to the Bible—show them the history of the two greatest temptations the world has ever known—that of Eve in the Old Testament, and of the second Adam in the New. Strive by these records to prove to them the devil's personality— and they will say, "Oh! yes. But we don't believe the Bible is anything more than a garbled version of the Indian or Persian 'Vedas.'"

What is to be done with minds in this state? —One only hope is left to us, and that is prayer. On women especially is this duty laid—to pray— to suffer—to immolate themselves—so that their prayers and their sacrifices may mount up to heaven and intercede for their husbands, their children, and their brothers, before the throne of God.

Most beautifully has Monseigneur de Mermillod shown us the three fundamental points on which Christianity must rest—Bethlehem, Nazareth, and Calvary—poverty, work, and suffering. And he has told us, likewise, how we may practise these three things—even though we may be, of what are called the " upper classes "—by lives of self-devotion and self-sacrifice.

We may practise poverty, by denying ourselves all superfluous luxuries. Work, by labouring for the sick, the sorrowful, the widows, the orphans— by our personal service—by our influence—by the employment of all those talents which God has given us on their behalf. Suffering, not only by offering up to God for others whatever pain He may be pleased to inflict, but also by voluntarily taking upon ourselves such expiation as may be possible to us, for the sins of unbelief, the blasphemous words and thoughts of those near and dear to us, or around us.

Looking in these days at the youth who are growing up, and living day by day in utter denial of God's revealed truths, we are tempted sometimes to despair and to exclaim: " When the Lord cometh shall He find Faith on the earth ?"

Yet, let us not lose heart. God is on our side. And if we be but in earnest, persevering and faithful to the duties of that great apostolate to which Mgr. Mermillod considers all women are now called, we shall win in the end. But to ensure this, we must first cleanse our own hearts. We must be united to God in love and in prayer. The whole secret of our influence over the souls of others lies in this—without it our words will be unprofitable and vain.

Such is the teaching of the book before us—such its great and holy lessons. May we all lay them to heart, and endeavour, each in our different spheres, to labour for souls. " *Da mihi animam !*" was the cry of St. Francis Xavier, thirsting for the glory of God through the salvation of men. And this thirst we, too, must feel, if we would be the children of the same Father, partakers of the same promises, and heirs together of the inheritance of the saints in light.

MARY ELISABETH HERBERT.

LONDON, *Easter*, 1874.

CONTENTS.

PAGE

EIGHTH CONFERENCE.

NINTH CONFERENCE.

TENTH CONFERENCE.

ELEVENTH CONFERENCE.

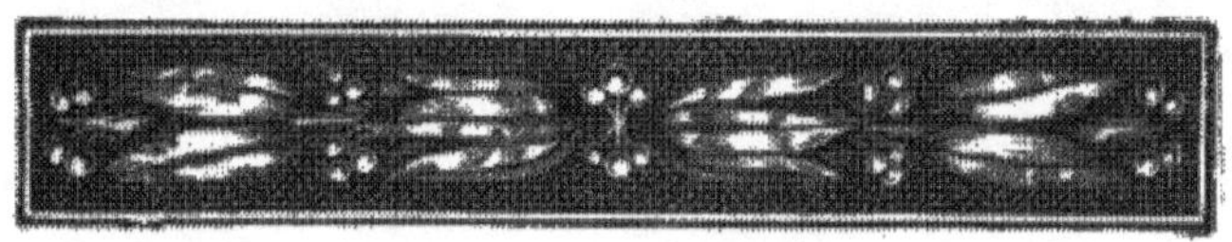

The Supernatural Life.

"To me to live is Christ."—Philippians i. 21.

TWO years ago, my sisters, I told you why there was a special retreat for you: it is because the word of God, as it is generally preached from our pulpits, however eloquent, however devoted and zealous the preacher, is often fruitless, because it is addressed to every one; because it has no speciality. You, my sisters, require something more intimate, something more applicable to your different positions; and even that is not enough; often you want something yet more individual, something which will touch your hearts; and it is in the hope of satisfying this double necessity that the retreat now about to commence is given.

It is not, therefore, my intention to preach to you

the great truths of Christianity, such as you hear them in your own quiet parish churches when you go to hear the word of God. My wish is to complete now the instructions I began two years ago, and thus to revive and renew, so to say, your fervour and your zeal.

And retreats are of great use to you, my sisters ; every soul requires them, from time to time. Jesus Christ, and He is our great example, passed thirty years of His life in retirement and three only in activity. And you, my sisters, you have but a few days of retreat in the midst of years of activity ! After our Lord's death, the Holy Spirit entered into the tabernacle and into the life of the Church. That is the silent life of retreat. Secular clergy, priests, spouses of Jesus Christ, all ought to withdraw themselves every year for a certain time behind the cloister walls, in order to refresh their souls and reflect on the solemn truths of religion.

And you, my sisters, still more require the wonderful discipline of silence. That power of silence ! Do you know that it is said in the Scriptures that silence is the devotion of the just ? Have you ever noticed the eloquent power of silence ? Of course you can never have entered a Trappist monastery; but if you have ever been on the threshold of their cloister, you may have seen pass before you on his road to the fields, a man clothed in serge, bearing on his shoulders some implement of labour, his lips sealed as if with a signet ring of silence, and his eyes raised to heaven with that grave, recollected look which proceeds from I know not what depth of soul.

Silence has passed by ! That man is conversing with God alone ; he lets the bustle of the world die away at his feet ; he sees his fellow-men expire before him. Oh ! there is indeed great strength in silence !

During this retreat, my sisters, let me entreat of you to try to have this strength ; learn to be silent, turn a deaf ear to the voices of the world around you, listen to the holy word of God.

Two years ago when speaking to you my thoughts were summed up in these words : "On the understanding and direction of life." I then told you that the question was how to understand and to govern your lives, and I tried to explain to you these two ideas. There is a third point which is as it were a step in advance; I have already prepared you for it. It is not only necessary that you should understand the great object of your lives; you must also sanctify them. And it is on the subject of a holy life, or to make use of a theological expression which will explain my meaning, it is on the subject of *the supernatural life* that I propose to speak to you now.

Yes, my sisters, God requires from us a supernatural life. Two years ago I said to you: " What, after all, is life? a flame, burning rapidly away between the cradle and the grave."

Have you from time to time meditated seriously on the mystery of life? It is a subject on which science is powerless; and philosophy even succumbs, wandering on from doubt to doubt, and from inquiry to inquiry. In poetry, life takes the form sometimes of a funereal dirge, sometimes of a smile, sometimes of a shining star, sometimes of a passing cloud. But real life!—who has ever explained it? To you, for instance, does it not present itself as a profound mystery?

God takes possession of us in a state of chaos, without asking for our consent; He calls us into life and casts us for a moment upon this grain of sand which we call the earth ; we appear on it, and we endeavour to shine and to distinguish ourselves. God then takes us back, He lays His hand upon us : where will He send us to ? Will it be to the chaos out of which He called us? will it be to a place of torment ? or are we to be for ever united with Him ? Human reason gives way in the face of this unfathomable mystery, and like a child who falls on its knees it clasps its hands and cries out to God : " O my God, reveal to me the secret of life !"

But, my sisters, it is not enough to understand life, we must utilize and govern it; we must, so to say, take it up in our hands, we must organize it, and make it into a note which shall be in unison with the general harmony of creation. We must so fashion our life that it may not be like a shell, which bursts and then disappears, like a light which only shines for a moment, or like a dead leaf which the wind carries away.

Do you know what it is which always strikes me at the hour of death ? for it has often been my lot to assist those who are struggling in the agonies of the last great battle. It is to see what a fund of understanding there generally is in the human soul, what a passionate desire it possesses of love and devotedness, and how all this has often remained fruitless and useless, like a roll of stuff in the corner of a shop which has remained untouched by any one.

Yes, at the hour of death, one again and again finds souls which are indeed like rolls of stuff (forgive me the familiarity of the simile), souls who have never felt, but who ought, so to say, to have been unrolled and expanded by their own natural and legitimate development. And thus life, when it is neither directed nor understood, is rendered useless; it then becomes an empty and a barren life, and this is a terrible thing to think of.

By the side of these marred and incomplete lives, we must, however, confess that we do find some which have been thoroughly and masterfully understood and regulated. We find souls who know how to control their passions, and to conquer their weaknesses; still these are not sanctified lives.

How many empty souls are there not in our own time! There are souls which allow themselves to be engrossed with the merest trifles; by some slight annoyance, some pleasure, or even an article of dress. These things are enough to satisfy them. And if you deprive them of what seems to be the object and the aim of their existence, you will find nothing but a void.

My wish, therefore, in this respect is to teach you how to employ your lives by filling them with Almighty God, and with the supernatural strength of our Lord Jesus Christ.

God requires, as I have said, a supernatural life in our souls. Why is this? And what, especially in these days, are the chief obstacles to this supernatural life? These are the two points upon which we will meditate together. God requires this supernatural life, because God had a divine plan. God does not act by caprice, God is Infinite Wisdom, as He is the *one Infinite Being;* He is beauty, as He is goodness; He is love, as He is light. When God acts exteriorly, when He makes use of His creative power, He has a plan. He leaves His eternal silence, He calls forth the world by His omnipotent word, and, stretching the sky as a tent over our heads, He places us between heaven and earth. He has willed that man should be created to glorify God.

Man exists only in order that he may glorify Him. Every other aim of humanity is a deception and a snare. Humanity was only created in order that it might become a sort of hymn of praise to God. You, my sisters, only exist to form, as it were, individual notes in the eternal concert, taking up, so to say, the chant which every blade of grass, every star, the sun, and all the luminaries of the firmament, are for ever and ever repeating in their daily rotation, " Glory be to God !"

Every created being who does not recognize this one great object of life is a being out of place. You must often have met in the world, in these days more than ever, beings such as these. Who has not again and again come across these sickly and miserable existences, souls weighed down by the battle of life, by the struggle against poverty, souls full of boundless aspirations and insatiable cravings ? When an existence has not God and His glory for its aim it is an existence out of place, it is no longer in harmony with the divine plan. God only created the world in order to further His glory. Therefore it is that the saints had the thought of eternity ever before their minds.

" We only exist for God," they were wont to say, "and for His glory alone ; that is the supreme aim of our lives."

Doubtless, God acts for our happiness ; but our happiness is also His glory. And when, turning away from happiness by the use of that fatal privilege, the law of our own liberty (a law as terrible as it is glorious), we refuse to glorify Him, we still show forth His glory, inasmuch as we manifest His justice.

God requires no other object in His work than Himself. We are creatures sprung from His omnipotence in order to be united to Him eternally : we go from Him to Him. Our life ought to be as a flame detached, in one sense, from this central fire of life ; rapidly it runs along, and returns to it again. God is the Beginning and the End : in the words of Holy Scripture, He is the Alpha and the Omega. Such is the scheme devised by divine wisdom.

It is a sad delusion, my sisters, not to understand this divine scheme, and the place which you occupy in it. When God made the world, He heard the voice of the soul, the sounds of the lower spheres ;

but you have not understood this. And yet, this cry of the soul, the cry of the child, saying, " My father ;" the cry which rejoices the mother's heart, when, some few months after its birth, she sees the fragile creature to which she has given life awakening to consciousness, and restless and unquiet, until, out of the depths of its being, comes forth this cry, " My mother !" This is the first throb, the first engendering of a thought. And, my sisters, God willed, likewise, to hear the beatings of the soul ; He desired to come into contact with creation in the depths of the harmony of the universe. God created man that He might listen to the human voice ascending on high above the stars, and crying, " My Father !" God, therefore, inclined His ear ; He bowed down the heavens ; He willed to hear, and He heard.

But, inasmuch as it was not God's Will that this voice should be a solitary one, He called forth woman that she might be united to man. One who was both a poet and a very eloquent bishop has expressed this idea most admirably as follows. God created both the major and the minor key, he says, for He joined together power and weakness, strength and tenderness, that from them might come forth the great hymn of humanity singing the praises of God. Woman was intended, in one sense, to take her share in the accomplishment of this design. She was to carry it out, and to be man's helpmeet and his partner. Both, in fact, being created by the divine hand for the one object of giving glory to God!

To give glory to God! What a grand vocation! Do you not feel that therein is one of your greatest joys? I appeal to your maternal feelings, to the recollections of a mother's heart. If it has ever happened to you to see one of your children praised and honoured, do you not remember the pure and overwhelming joy which came over you? When, for instance, in a distribution of prizes, you watched your child, at the age, perhaps, of twelve or fifteen, timidly advancing from amongst his companions, looking round to catch his mother's eye, and then, with a hesitating, faltering step, coming forward to receive the little laurel crown awarded to his diligence or his good conduct, oh, how your mother's heart beat, and how happy you were at the triumph of your son! And it is some-

thing, certainly, to have been instrumental in the
honour and glory of one's own child; but to give
glory to our Father, to Him Who created us, to
Him Whom the whole universe adores, to glorify
Almighty God, such is our grand, our sublime
vocation.

But besides giving glory to God, it is also our
duty to act and to work. It is a very great mistake
to think that before the Fall we were not meant to
labour. Before the Fall we were destined to work,
and you, therefore, women of the world, who do
nothing, you are not living according to the law
either before or after the Fall; you are outside the
existence of the terrestrial paradise, and of the
existence of humanity; your lives are neither in
accordance with primitive humanity, with fallen
humanity, nor with humanity restored.

Idleness is the most terrible thing in the world.
Everything in nature has its own work to do. The
grain of sand seeks its cohesion with another grain;
the spider weaves its web; the eagle sores into the
sky; the sap rises in the plants; the sun sends
forth his rays upon the most elevated regions of the
globe. All nature is at work; and in the midst of

this universal activity we dare not be idle. We were created to glorify God and to labour for Him.

In this primary design of God you were meant to develop your understanding, your character, your heart, your soul—you were intended to work; and this was the work which God would accomplish through and in you. This was His original design ; you were to see God face to face. Not, indeed, that He created us to attain unto Him by our own strength ; we do not know Him, and as I proceed I shall have to show you that one of the great sorrows of the priesthood of our own time is to feel that Christianity is so little understood, so little appreciated, and especially that it penetrates so little into the depths of the soul. Remember, God created us for Himself; but another element beyond the human element was necessary. We are not only creatures with a physical organization, endowed with living souls, but above and beyond the body which contains the living soul, there is a supernatural element, *i.e.,* grace.

A holy father used to say, " A Christian is a soul within a body, and God within a soul."

As a body without a soul becomes a corpse,

which goes on from one state of decay to another, from corruption to corruption, until it becomes that for which human language has no name, so a soul without God is a soul which is no longer Christian.

There is an element which comes directly from God, an element which man cannot produce by his own will or wish : this element, which is a gratuitous gift of God, is grace ; it is God in us; it is Jesus Christ in us. That which makes the life of my body, that which kindles my eyes, that which gives power to my hands, which moves my lips, and which trembles on my tongue, is the soul within me. . . . My soul can reach your souls. Had I no soul, I should return to silence and to immobility. The soul that is without God, is not alive, but is void, dead or dying. Such is the supernatural element which God has given us; God within us, this is the supernatural life.

And not only is this the original design, but at the same time it is the end of our being.

You may do what you will, my sisters, you have known it again and again, and your own weakness has surely borne witness to the fact that rest is not for this earth ; that this life is not the final aim ;

life, even the most eventful, is not the real end of existence. You have felt this—life is not life—we are but travellers here below; everything wearies us; everything brings uncertainty and satiety. But the day will come when the soul, having accomplished the end for which she was destined, will at length see God. When, like a veil of flesh, this body shall be put off, and the soul forced from her mortal shroud, shall pass from the darkness of this world to eternal light, then shall she see God face to face. This heart, this poor, inconstant, palpitating heart shall feel its God, and shall drink in the intoxicating stream of supernal joys of entrancing delight.

We are destined to see God, to love Him, and to possess Him, just as your eyes are in possession of light, your heart of affection; just as your body possesses the nourishment which is the aliment of your existence. You are destined to live in God. Your real life is a supernatural light, it is something altogether apart from this world. Hence do we find everywhere trouble and anguish and pain and universal complaining.

You well know the cry sent forth by the whole

of nature, and which has so well been called melancholy. This melancholy exists in everything throughout creation. For here below our existence is incomplete, and even when we have attained to the supernatural life, we still see it but dimly and hazily through the veils and shadows and mysteries of our poor humanity.

Have you ever come in contact with souls who were leading a supernatural life ?   Have you ever seen a saint ?   I have known saints.   Oh, if you could but have seen their life !

When, as you were wont, you went a few miles from here to visit that venerable old curé, whose life was a living miracle, in his presence you felt the power of the soul piercing through his thoughts, and under that tongue, rude and uncultured as it might be, you still heard the seethings of the fire within that mighty heart ; you felt that here was a soul living in God and through God.

What do we mean by the supernatural life ?

It is said of the venerable Pontiff, who governs the Church, that he lives entirely in the supernatural. The noise of men, the turmoil of this world, have no power to move him.   A few months ago I was with him—at his feet—listening to the beating of his heart. But one idea absorbed his mind, and that was to know whether saints were now being formed in the world.

We are full of excitement, and therefore we believe that we have life; we see modern society struggling in feverish activity; we fly over distance on our iron roads; we torture this little globe of ours; we gain great victories over matter; we make great advances in trade; all this is true. But is this all? God sees our efforts, He hears the noise of our machinery; but do you know what He will do with this poor earth if, at His coming, He finds on it none that are saints? He will take it and break it in pieces like a potter's vessel.

The earth only exists to bring forth saints. Centuries roll on only in order that saints may be formed. Saints are the effect of the supernatural life in the soul, the result, in fact, of God's divine plan. You cannot change this admirable design of the supreme Ruler. Consequently, the end of your creation, the whole order of things, is super-natural life within you.

Have you ever thought much of this? Listen to

the turmoil of the world. Are there many Christians in our days? The women of our time, they have a certain life, it is true; they have a religious faith which shows itself in activity, and in self-sacrifice; but women in general, if you will allow me the expression, may be said to let themselves live rather than to live. They give way to the passing impressions of each day, to every fresh emotion of the heart; fickle and inconstant they are perpetually influenced by whatever happens to move or to strike them; in a word they let themselves live rather than live. Or, do they live that life of the understanding which aims at knowing God through faith, that life of the affections which tries to know Him through love, that love of the will which seeks to know Him through grace and through conscience, which desires His divine presence within the soul?

I implore you to consider this; now is the time for saints, for holy souls. More than ever God calls you; He invites, He entreats you to come to Him!

Oh! I know full well the objections, the difficulties which present themselves; I know how the

world and the devil may attack you. Remember
what a holy priest once said to a woman of the
world, who was hesitating between God and
vanity :

"My child, do what you will, and try what you
will, the world will ever be against you."

And so, indeed, it is, my sisters. If you are
Christians the world will call you *dévotes*; if you
are worldly, it will still find fault with you. The
world is for ever complaining ; for its business is to
accuse and to insult ; never can it be a soil which
will bring forth great souls.

And you must co-operate in this divine scheme.
If you do not sing God's praises, if you do not give
Him glory, if you are at war with Him, sooner
or later He will take possession of you in spite of
yourself; no longer, indeed, will it be through the
liberty of your will, but through the tortures of
your conscience ; then will you be, so to say, a discord, but a discord which He will compel to enter
into His divine composition ; you will glorify Him
in spite of yourself.

But you have come here to seek your sanctification ; you wish to have the supernatural life within

you. It is your aim in this retreat. Let me, then, tell you what are the obstacles to this supernatural life within you.

I know not if I have already alluded to a fact which has again and again been repeated to me by men of the world. They maintain that this is a moment of great mental conflict, of great intellectual struggle. It is terrible to think of the sufferings produced by all the uncertainties, the wearing investigations, and the often fruitless researches in which men involve themselves in matters of faith.

I know nothing which is at once so great and so sad as such a moral strife in the souls of men; there is nothing greater than to see a soul make effort upon effort, and rise again at last, in spite of repeated falls, for to fall is human, to rise again angelic. The soul emerges from the deadly fight crushed and bleeding; and the heart, tortured as it has been by the miseries and the disappointments of this world, is henceforth yielded once for all to Jesus Christ. Doubtless this is a supreme effort, it is the grand side of the work of Christians.

· But side by side with this, there is a sadder spectacle! There are doubting, questioning souls, souls

who are for ever saying, " Could I but believe!
happy are you who have Christian convictions!"
How often in every class of society do we not hear
this lamentable cry : " Happy are you who have
faith !"

It is the same cry that issued from the lips of one
who, we are told, returned from Paris to his native
valley in the Jura.   He had tasted the pleasures of
worldly success, he had been the object of admiration to a delighted audience, who could not sufficiently applaud his learning and his philosophy ;
yet what are his reflections on finding himself once
more in his own village ?

" I went to Mass on Sunday," he says, "and as
I sat down on the tottering, time-worn wooden
bench, my heart was moved ; nothing was changed !
It was the same congregation, the same good old
priest who preached from the pulpit, his hair had .
whitened, but he taught the same faith, said the
same Credo, and was listened to by the same
audience ; the same simple pictures hung on the
walls of that village church, the same heads were
bowed down to receive the priestly benediction ;
nothing was changed, only over my own heart a

change had come. . . . When I was fifteen I believed; one day the wind of incredulity blew upon me, and my life of faith, so happy, so serene, was destroyed."

What a dreadful moment! he looked into his soul . . . there was nothing of which he could take hold; then bursting into tears he fell on his knees, and, clasping his hands, exclaimed,

"How miserable all this learning has made me! for it has taught me to reason, and to reason is to doubt, and to doubt is to suffer. My soul is filled with sadness, so that neither the beauty around me, nor the flowers, nor the sweet songs of the birds have the power to touch me. Oh! my God, give me my mother's faith!"

Such is, more or less, the universal cry of humanity; everywhere around us are lamentations . and complaints!

One great objection which I often hear brought forward in religious discussions, by those who have not our faith—by Protestants—is this:

"Your Christianity," they say, "does not produce solid fruit; you have, it is true, many zealous religious, you often give us examples of wonderful self-sacrifice; but has Christianity really penetrated into the soul, is the root very deep?"

Nor can we deny that there is something true in this. People are terribly superficial in these days! their life is one of sentiment or of activity; Christianity has not penetrated deeply into their heart. It is often only a juxtaposition between the soul and Christianity; whereas Christianity ought to be the very sap and marrow of the soul.

My sisters, you believe in two fundamental facts, which are the basis, so to say, of all that ever happened in the world; you believe in the fact of the Fall, and in the fact of our Redemption; you believe that man fell, and that he was redeemed.

Are these two all-important facts the very compass of your life? Are they its light and its brightness? Do you form your judgments by the light of these two facts? Do you believe that there is a curse upon man, that there is a curse upon the earth? Do you believe that man was redeemed by the blood of Jesus Christ? Are these two great events in the history of humanity your starting points, and do they influence all that you do and think?

' But there are objections, you say, to all this. True, there are ordinary objections and obstacles, and again such as belong especially to the present time. Now ordinary obstacles may be said to exist in every living soul, and the first, according to my judgment, is religious ignorance. Religious ignorance is a terrible feature in our own time. How few have really had proper instruction in religious doctrine! Do you want a proof of this?

I have been an attentive listener to the recent decree of our Holy Father the Pope. You know what disturbance it created throughout the world— in France, in Italy, in Russia, in America—everywhere. Well, when I saw this decree so misunderstood, I said to myself:

"Where, after all, is Christianity, when pontifical words can be so misconstrued, so little appreciated?"

Many there are who do not in the least understand the meaning of the decree; and yet our Holy Father the Pope has but announced the fact that there is no kind of society, just as there is no human soul, which can exist without Jesus Christ.

It is a most simple, we might almost say, a commonplace thing ; and yet the enlightened Christians of the nineteenth century, the Christians who think so much of progress, of development, the Christians who wish to direct the bishops and the whole papacy, do not understand this one primary lesson : that Jesus Christ must be the life of souls, as He is the life of nations ; the corner-stone of our families, as well as that of our consciences. This simple truth has been ignored. Oh ! my sisters, what ignorance there is in the world !

And this ignorance extends itself even to questions which may be found in the catechism. Who, now-a-days, has any belief in the supernatural ? Hardly any one. And yet every life, in order to be a true one, ought to be a supernatural life !

Now, it is the object of this retreat to bring once more before your minds primary truths such as these.

Real Christian truth is a noble and a grand thing—who shall deny it ? Yet I speak with sadness ; for how often do I not see people—women especially—giving their whole heart, their feelings, their entire devotion to some ideal, beautiful and poetical, it is true, but which yet bears upon it the stamp and impress of humanity? But you, my sisters, must not rest there. Look above, take your flight on high, rise to the incomparable grandeur of Christian truth; take your flight on high. "Sursum corda." Lift up your hearts and learn to study the wonderful splendours of Christianity.

If you would destroy the effects of religious ignorance, devote yourselves to the study of Christianity, which contains unequalled beauty.

The idea that the grand traditions of Christian and of domestic life should, as it were, find their expression in the divine liturgy and in the pages of Holy Writ, is no longer understood by any one.

Religious ignorance is, therefore, evidently one great obstacle to an understanding of the supernatural life. If I descend to familiar and practical details I might ask who, amongst the women of the world, has even re-read her catechism (except the catechism of perseverance); this catechism which your bishops labour at so carefully; this book once so popular; this book which used to be found in every home, and which every mother formerly taught her child herself? And yet, my sisters, you are the guardians, the natural protectors of your families. If Christian truth declines in your own souls, it will be the same in the hearts of your sons and of your brothers. I repeat, therefore, the first and the chief obstacle to the supernatural life is religious ignorance.

The second obstacle, which I will define by a true but sharp word, is the cowardice of our hearts.

The heart is full of cowardice, a cowardice which it justifies, which it excuses even; a cowardice which takes many forms, but which is still cowardice.

Our Master has said,

"Deny yourselves, mortify yourselves, forsake yourselves; he that will be My disciple, let him take up his cross and follow Me."

Which of us is not a coward in following this rule of Christian life? You, who some years ago returned to God, instead of ascending to the supernatural, have been dragging on listlessly, feebly, tepidly along the path of duty. You did but exchange one kind of weakness, one kind of cowardice for another; when you belonged to the world you were cowardly towards it; now you are cowardly towards yourselves. You will be cowardly in old age if you are cowardly in maturity and in youth. You must arm yourselves with holy energy, with real strength, with saintly courage for the battle of life. Cowardice of heart is a great obstacle ; we must compel our heart to rise ; we must, as it were, take hold of it with both hands.

I know that cowardice grows upon us rapidly, and with cowardice comes illusions. We sometime hear it said,

" It is enough for me to have the lesser virtues, to be quiet and easy-going ; enough if I lead a harmless life, and do no great wrong ; it is not every one who can aspire to heroic virtue."

Virtue, my sisters, is of every state. Take St. Francis of Sales as your light, your guide ; he preached renunciation. It is not the renunciation of happiness which I am recommending — self-renunciation is not the renunciation of happiness. You yourselves are often the chief obstacle to your own happiness ; it is not always those who are around you. You complain that it is your children, your husbands, your relations ; no, you are yourselves the obstacle to your own happiness. There are hidden weaknesses within you ; you are wanting in bravery of heart. This is the one great work you have to accomplish in order that you may acquire the virtues of which you stand in need.

The third obstacle may, perhaps, proceed from your family.

I have already said that, in the divine scheme, you were to be united to man in order to promote God's glory. But, alas, man does not help you in this; man has too much to do. See what domestic life is in the present day! People in the world are quite ready to help you when it is a question of deciding on a stuff for a dress, or of arranging a party, or of settling about your children's future; but will they help you when it is a question of serving God? When, in a Christian family, you begin to speak about working for the glory of God, you are met with smiles, and looks of bewilderment. You might be talking about some unknown thing in a strange tongue.

And yet your family should be a help to direct you in the best way of glorifying God, a stay to support and strengthen you when you lament your failures in His service. Again, in your family you ought to find encouragement in this service. But, alas! you do not always find these things. The place in the divine scheme assigned to woman exists no longer in its completeness; you have neither help, nor stay, nor encouragement. It is sad to say this. Supernatural light has penetrated but little into Christian families.

There is a fourth obstacle.

Society is built up irrespective of the supernatural. For the last three centuries it has been formed irrespective of Jesus Christ. Laws and customs have been constituted without regard to Him. Men have rejected the supernatural in the construction of society, they have rejected that which alone could bind it together. You live in a thoroughly human, in a thoroughly earthly atmosphere, of which you inhale the poisonous breath. Therefore is it that a time of retreat is necessary for you. In these few days of silence and recollection you will understand the greatness of the supernatural life in the soul. I hope to implant within you a strong purpose for good.

At the end of the last retreat, there were some who thoroughly understood that their lives must be sanctified and transformed under the action of divine grace; that life, in fact, can only be complete when the soul is under the influence of God.

I will conclude by an illustration taken from the "Confessions" of St. Augustine. I have often quoted some of his beautiful words during his intercourse with his mother. There are some admirable passages in his "Confessions."

When St. Augustine was himself hesitating and vacillating, undecided whether to give himself to God or to the world, one hand uplifted to heaven, the other still pointing to the earth—and which of us has not had moments of uncertainty, of hesitation and indecision, when one seems, as it were, to halt between God and the world?—it was at the very moment, I say, when St. Augustine was in one of those hours, which are often the crisis of a man's eternal destiny, that God granted him a vision.

When the soul has been faithful and true, God often comes to her aid in some unexpected manner. There appeared to Augustine a woman of dazzling brightness, bearing on her head a crown, and in her hands a sceptre. Behind her followed a solemn procession. There were children, young girls, young men, and old men. This woman was eternal

wisdom.   Augustine understood this, and she called
him to her.   "I drew near to her," he tells us,
"prostrating myself before her, yielding to the
fascination of her look; the magic of her words
entranced me. This woman said to me, 'Augustine,
these children, these virgins, these youths, these old
men, have struggled as much as thou hast. They
have learnt to overcome; but thou, thou art a
coward.'" Terrified and crushed by these words,
Augustine rises, clasps his hands, and says, "I will
do what these have done!" And, with rapid
strides, he rushes forth into the paths of holiness
and truth.

My sisters, you will hear from my lips the voice
of eternal wisdom, the words of Jesus Christ Himself. He will reveal to you your weakness, your
hesitations, your uncertainties, and you will have
the courage to arise and say, "My soul shall be no
longer void, my life shall be no longer useless. My
soul shall be no longer dead. My life shall be full,
my soul shall live. Not upon a handful of earth,
not on a dream, an ideal, but on a reality, on the
fulness of God."

May you, then, my sisters, live upon God; may

you understand this holy life ; may it be poured out upon you abundantly at this present time ; and may you ever have courage to carry out the sweet and blessed requirements of the divine life.

Supernatural Life through Jesus Christ.

"Vivit in me Christus"—"Christ liveth in me."—Galatians ii. 20.

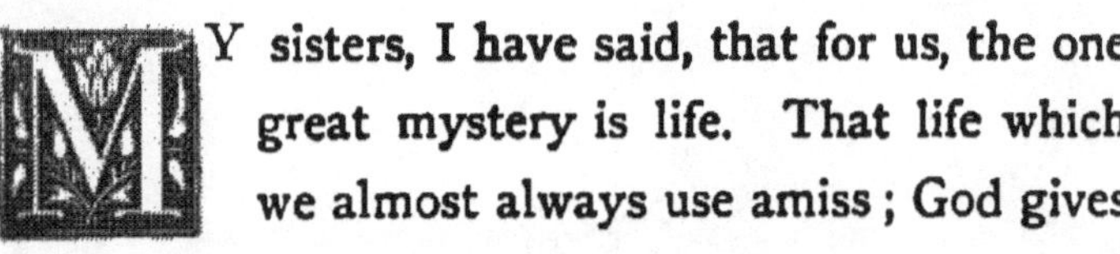

MY sisters, I have said, that for us, the one great mystery is life. That life which we almost always use amiss; God gives it to us rich in seed, and we return it to Him marred and without fruit. We mingle tears with its smiles, and often we make it as empty as our own souls. The highest knowledge is the comprehension and the mastery of life. And what, after all, is this but a purely human and natural attainment; an earthly science, in fact? for the heathen themselves thought they understood the object of life, they wished to render it useful.

But, since the coming of Jesus Christ, since the word of God has bowed the everlasting hills, since the time when He took upon Him our flesh, there is for us an onward step to be made. It is no longer enough to understand the meaning of life, and to govern and utilize it; we are also called upon to sanctify it. Every soul which does not take this step is still outside the circle of Christianity, outside of its teaching, an alien from the law of Faith, and from the Blood of Redemption. You must therefore sanctify your lives.

The order of things into which God has called us is a supernatural one. The divine plan does not consist merely in a terrestrial organization; it is a power above created things; it is a supreme goal, a final term which has no solution in this world. There still remains that which I have called the supernatural, the order increate; and although modern science, and that contemporary incredulity which arrogates to itself the dignity of criticism, has dared to say, in every kind of way, " The supernatural does not exist because it is outside of the things of sense," it is none the less true, that beyond the natural world, and the laws of the natural world, the supernatural does exist; it is the power of the uncreated, a power above what is created, even as God is above man ; God Who is the essence of supernatural being.

God is Himself the end of His own works. For since the world is of His own creation, it follows that He is the object of His own operations, He must therefore of necessity be their final aim, for He can only act for Himself. What indeed can be the end of God, but Himself ? As we come forth from Him, so must we return to Him.

In calling us into this world, His primary intention was that our existence should be devoted to His glory and to the fulfilment of His purposes. It is but an illusion to imagine that before the fall we were not intended for action; but that life in the terrestrial paradise was to be a state of mere passive immobility, that, in fact, Adam and Eve were destined to perpetual contemplation.

No, the full powers of their mind, of their whole organization were to be called into play, and thus by the complete development of their being to give glory to God. They were to be united, Adam being the head, representing strength ; Eve, the helpmeet, or weakness : and thus was formed that first family on earth, which was to give a name both to the herb of the field and to the stars of the firmament.

Such was the object of creation. This object was destroyed, and the original plan cast aside. Then God came and made it anew; hence He is our Redeemer. He took up the ruins and formed thereof a new order of things, wherein was to be a harmony for which no human tongue has any name; the soul was clothed with Jesus Christ, and received power to sing the glory of God.

It is of this power of Jesus Christ within you, my sisters, that I would speak this morning. This evening and to-morrow, we will examine the obstacles which either your own minds or the spirit of the world oppose to it. But what I wish to impress upon you to-day is, that the aim of your life must be to put on Jesus Christ.

If I can but make you understand this great truth you will be raised above the earth, you will accomplish your *sursum corda*, you will take your flight, soaring above to those fair regions so rich in beauty and in sweetness, and taste the fulness of their entrancing beauty.

Let man then, in imitation of the angels, ascend again to God, and seek to grasp Him in intimate union, until in Him he finds happiness and strength; until in fact he has, so to say, made God His own.

I spoke yesterday of the primitive plan. God's first thought was the glorification of His own Being, but man's first thought was rebellion against God. All history may be summed up in these words: the voice of God requiring man to serve and praise Him; and the voice of man refusing to obey. The great conflicts of this world, the great battle-fields of the earth, the ceaseless strife of opinions, all these are but repetitions of the ever-recurring struggle for mastery between the divine and the human, between Jesus Christ and man.

The first step of man was the fall, that fall which with a smile we may deny, but which none the less we see imprinted everywhere on creation, indelibly stamped thereon by the ravages and the convulsions of ages.

The fall is written in unmistakable characters alike upon the body and upon the soul. Upon the body in the diseases to which it is subject; upon the soul in the sorrows of the heart, the tortures of conscience, the terrors of the imagination, and the anguish of sensitive feelings. Again, the fall shows itself in our homes in the disappointments we meet with; in society by the internal storms which rend it; in the world by the struggles which it necessitates; in souls by the eclipse of faith which is the forerunner of the end of all things.

It may be said that the world and the soul are two pages of one great book wherein may be read the fall of man and the decadence of humanity. Now, when you have thus apprehended the fall, you come to another problem, the restoration of the ruin. You feel that you yourself are but a ruin; you would not destroy it, and yet you are unable to rebuild the edifice according to the original plan. The architect must descend and come forward; and this architect is Jesus Christ.

That I may make this thought intelligible to you and bring it home in a way which shall be both luminous and tangible to your understandings, let me take an illustration from human life.

We will suppose that you are twenty: you look

around you; you feel isolated. The affection of your mother, the charms of society no longer suffice you. You feel that you have a family right to a place in the world, and you demand it. You are in search of four things: a head, first of all, because we are not placed in this world to be independent. Next, you seek an ideal; it has been your dream from the earliest dawn of your life. You look for a stay upon which you may lean; and lastly, you look for a friend, into whose heart you may pour forth the treasures of your own. This is what you feel the want of when first your heart awakens; you long to wing your flight to another home from that in which your first years of childhood and youth were spent. You seek, I repeat, these four things; a head, an ideal, a stay, and a friend.

I do not say that you have met with them. Yet do we constantly find the sweet name of sister and of spouse applied to woman in holy writ. God grant that she may consider herself the spouse of Jesus Christ! We do not give this name only to those who, in convents or before the altar, forsake all that they have, and by one supreme sacrifice devote themselves to poverty and virginity: although such are indeed the spouses of Jesus Christ. But all Christian souls are spouses of the Living God; you confess it sometimes yourselves in the words used at communion, in that prayer which seems like an echo of the words of the liturgy.

Jesus wills to be the spouse of every human soul, presenting Himself to us in this fourfold form; as a head, an ideal, a stay, a friend. Thus does Jesus Christ offer Himself to each one of us.

Well, my sisters, this is what you do not find in the world. Does this world even offer to you a head capable of governing or of understanding you? An ideal! You think to have formed one—a few short hours—and it falls from its pedestal. A stay! How often does not the arm fail you on which you hope to rest. A friend? No, it is but the juxtaposition of two lives; not the intimacy, the transfusion of two hearts; and if there be no such transfusion, your heart must have its sorrows.

The human soul is an orphan in this world. Who can understand the soul?—the mother? the husband? Some brilliant and fleeting gleam of the mind may sometimes be understood, or some gentle affections of the heart; but the soul, who shall understand her? The soul is ever more or less orphaned, more or less widowed in this world! The soul, in fact, needs a head, for the orphan and the widow need a head; and this head is Jesus Christ. He came into this world to be its Sovereign and its Ruler—He came to reign. In His very cradle, and even before He was called blessed in His mother's womb, He was sung by the prophets, "He shall come the Son of David; He shall sit upon His throne; He shall be King!"

The prophets had called Him King; as King the angel announces Him; and when guided by the star the magi seek Him. When the star disappears they still inquire,

"Where is the King of the Jews?"

And when on the cross, still the title is written over Him—He is, indeed, the King—He must reign, *oportet illum regnare.* When the people would give Him a crown, a fleeting royalty in this world, He withdraws to the desert; for He would reign only over souls, He wills no other sovereignty. The human soul must be the subject of Jesus Christ.

The soul cannot be independent. It is an illusion to believe in the independence of the soul. It must always depend either upon a person or upon a thing.

You live for an affection if you do not live for your ball-dresses. We often seem to trail our souls, just as that king of the air, the majestic eagle, trails his wing when maimed by some cruel shot. He falls; a slender thread suffices to hold him captive, and he drags himself wearily along in the mud or the dust of the road reddened with his blood.

Thus the soul, bruised by sin, falls like the royal bird from the heights, where, in the days of her innocence, she had dwelt; and held by the fetters of human weakness, she, too, lies grovelling in the low places of the earth, profaning her noblest faculties.

You have within you an inherent weakness which keeps you dependent; you cannot be independent; you are always under the dominion of some ruling fascination; you always will have a master; it may be the world, perhaps the most capricious of any; it may be vanity; it may be pleasure; but be assured of this, to some one sovereignty you must be subject.

Well, then, Jesus Christ claims this sovereignty, and when He wills to take possession of a soul what are not the struggles, the conflicts, the anguish through which He leads her! How does He at first trouble her, and having troubled, bruise and crush her; until at length He lifts her up again, and then the struggle over, the wounded soul regains her peace. If it has ever been our privilege to look into a soul of which Jesus Christ has taken possession, we have been conscious of something passing our comprehension, but which has been dimly revealed to us in the life-history of some of God's saints. Saint Paul, struck down on the road to Damascus, blinded, bruised, prostrate in the dust, lifts up his head and cries :

"Who art Thou ?"—"I am Jesus of Nazareth !"

Then the scales fall from his eyes; he is baptized and henceforth becomes one of the heroes of Christianity.

In the same way St. Augustine was drawn by the fleshly garment, as I reminded you yesterday.

Jesus Christ claims the sovereignity over us, but

He will have it absolute; He will accept no divided sovereignty; none of the semi-allegiance of hearts given indeed to God, but given partially; hearts which content themselves with offering Him the garment of outward profession, the showy formalism of religious observances; He claims an absolute sovereignty over the hearts of His creatures.

Has Jesus Christ this sovereignty over your thoughts? Does He regulate them? Is He the law of your understanding? Has He entire empire over your heart? Is He the source, the sap of your convictions? Does He rule your will, and is your will one with His?

Does He reign over your family, and through you does His rule embrace the circle of your influence, like an instrument of which the sound vibrates within the radius which surrounds it?

How rare is this sovereignty of Jesus Christ! How few souls accept His rule and His authority! There are even those who are frequent communicants, who consider themselves pious, who overdo themselves with devotion, and with devotional practices, yet the sovereignty of Jesus Christ is for them naught but a deception and a falsehood. There are even those who in the morning will go to Him for pardon, for a few moments' consolation, and who in the evening will bow down before other sovereignties, other masters more congenial to their weakness. How many are there, I repeat, who thus divide their lives?

There is but one royalty, the royalty of Jesus Christ; He must reign, *oportet illum regnare.* You must accept this royalty; it is the first word of redemption, of the supernatural order. Jesus Christ must reign over our hearts!

Think of this, my sisters, in these day of silence and recollection. Have you accepted the royalty of Jesus Christ? Is He the spouse of your soul? and do you glory in this sovereignty? To accept His reign, is to reign, as the Scriptures tell us, this alone is peace, this alone is happiness. He only has said these words:

"My yoke is sweet, and my burden light."

Everywhere else the yoke is hard and the burden heavy.

You are a heavy burden to yourselves; you often find it difficult to bear with yourselves.

Jesus Christ alone is the true Head, the true King, the true Sovereign ; He alone has spoken these words of tenderness and peace :

" My yoke is sweet, and my burden light."

But it is not enough that Jesus Christ should be our Head ; He must also become to you the type of your ideal, and your example.

God has created us for this supernatural end ; He has implanted this need within our inmost souls, and has placed before our eyes these words, so high in their requirement that I might well-nigh call them despairing :

" Be you, therefore, perfect, as also your Heavenly Father is perfect." " Be ye holy, even as I am holy."

We must accept this divine likeness, even though it be enough to make human nature despair. For we need an example, an ideal ; we need something which we can imitate. We need an ideal which we can love. Did we not feel this even in childhood ? I appeal to the recollections of your girlhood, in your day-dreams, harmless, innocent, pure as they were, did you not always picture to yourselves some unapproachable ideal ?

You decked it with all the riches of your imagination, the treasures of your heart; with fruitless and impotent efforts you vainly felt after this ideal, which you were ever pursuing and never able to reach.

We cannot find in ourselves all the beauty and satisfaction we look for; we are compelled to turn to an ideal which we may reproduce. It is necessary to us to reproduce it, for our nature is essentially imitative. Man will not be imitated, for he is proud; he is poor and his virtues are but limited; he imagines himself to be impoverished if he is reproduced, and in fact to rob him of his originality is to impoverish him.

Who, then, in this world shall be the ideal of humanity? Nowhere have you found it. You have seen, as Bossuet forcibly expresses it, that there is an imperfect side to all human wisdom; an imperfect side to all human beauty; you have found out that in all human intelligence there is ever a certain degree of obscurity; that there is some selfishness in all human affection; you have never, in fact, found perfection. In the Lord Jesus alone is the ideal. To me the ideal is the all-purifying fire of the Divinity, an idea to which I may return—I only hint at it now.

Have you ever reflected upon this strange mystery ? When a painter is taking a portrait, he seeks to hide, to veil, to soften certain faults in his model ; he tries to embellish the real features of the face of which he wishes to make a picture. Why ? Because his model is human, and humanity is always imperfect. But when the subject is Jesus Christ, admirable as the painting may be—the production, perhaps, of the highest genius, of a Rubens, a Raphael—yet will the very peasant, as he gazes at it, exclaim, " It is grand, but it is not Jesus Christ."

Humanity is ever fairer in a picture than in reality. With Jesus Christ it is different ; there you have an ideal above all humanity, something which never can be grasped, a sovereign power placed before our eyes in order that we may be perpetually striving to imitate it. An everlasting model, so perfect that it might almost make angels despair. And yet, when these celestial spirits contemplate the beauty of the Son of God, they are filled with feelings of tenderness and admiration.

But they do not feel discouraged. And this it is which proves the divinity of Jesus Christ. Because He is God, therefore did He take upon Himself our humanity, bringing Himself down to our level, to our comprehension, to the measure of our stature. We can imitate His meekness, we can follow the example of His mercy, we can practise His simplicity, we can share in His trust, we can try to identify ourselves with His devotedness. Oh, how beautiful is this ideal, how touching, how consoling!

How great is the privilege of endeavouring to imitate, to copy Jesus Christ! Have you studied this imitation of Him? Is it the foundation, the basis of all your meditations, the one ideal of your life? Do you study the actions of Jesus Christ? Do you read His Gospel? Do you strive to reproduce Jesus Christ within your own souls?

Oh, my sisters, were this indeed so, how would it not ennoble you, for your every thought would lift you up to God.

See, how paltry and earthly are the thoughts of the world. Even the great men of this world have their pettinesses and their weaknesses! By striving to reproduce Jesus Christ within you, your thoughts will rise, your heart and your feelings will be ennobled, your actions will be fruitful and generous; your whole life will be elevated, and raised above this world; you will find God, and it will be peace—peace in the forgetfulness of the past, while your heart and conscience will regain quietness and trust.

You see sometimes a storm sweep over the heavens, the tempestuous wind driving before it the clouds, and stirring up the waters on the surface of the earth. Suddenly the wind falls, a solemn stillness succeeds, and the troubled waters are calmed—they are once more limpid, transparent, clear as crystal, the sky is bright, and the image of the sun shining in the firmament is reflected in the splendour of the waters. The soul which has found her ideal in Jesus Christ is in the full enjoyment of peace; no clouds are above her, only the Sun of Righteousness. Look into the depths of that soul. You will see there reflected the image of Jesus Christ. Can aught be fairer? Great is the loyalty of the saint, great that of even the humblest

Christian, whose life reflects the image of Jesus Christ!

Look at that young girl, grown up in an humble position. She is but a simple country maiden; she cannot even read; she knows nothing of the world; its voice has not reached her ears, nor did she listen for it. But how great is her soul, how wonderful her thoughts! She has understood the aim of life; her heart is at rest: Jesus Christ abides with her even in the very homeliness of her existence. She is like the still waters, and the sun is reflected in a drop of water, as well as in the ocean. A soul may be as a drop of water in the world, or as an ocean, through its influence, if it animates a S. Geneviève, or a Joan of Arc; for the entire image of Jesus Christ is reflected in it.

Such, my sisters, is the ideal of humanity.

You search everywhere for your ideal! Well, you will be disappointed in youth as in old age. You pursue it everywhere, and nowhere will you find it save by the well of Jacob, where it was found by the woman of Samaria. You will find it also at the door of the Tabernacle, whence you will hear a voice, saying: "Oh, did you but know the gift of

God! Did you but know Jesus Christ, were He your model, then would you know real power, real strength." As Jesus Christ claims to be the guide and the model of your life, so would He be its stay.

We cannot bear to be alone; isolation weighs us down, solitude oppresses us. You are afraid of silence, you have a dread of encountering it face to face with your own selves. And it is, perhaps, this very horror which we have of isolation which induced Jesus Christ when on this earth to leave us Himself as our support ere He departed from it.

He desires to be to you a stay; such as a husband should be to a wife, or a father of a family to the members of his own household. He invites you to lean on His arm, so that you may bravely and valiantly pursue the path of duty and of right, and thus, in the end, gain your crown. Jesus Christ has given you what He calls grace; that is, an element uncreated and supernatural, which, in the divine order of things, may be compared to a ray of sunshine in the natural order. If the sun sends down a ray of its light into a dark room, every object in that room is lighted up; so is it in a soul, grace is the light which illuminates it, the heat which revives it: it is the one power which constitutes our stay and our support, and which directs us in the way of life. Such is the grace of God.

And this grace our Lord will ever give us. Do not trust to your own strength. You must have learnt this by sad experience. You fell into errors because you were left to yourselves. But our Lord will be even more than our support. He will be to us a friend.

Sometimes when I have been conversing with people who do not admit the truth of revelation, who do not believe, who recognize nothing but natural religion, I have said to them:

"But after all, what does natural religion give you? It can give you neither an ideal, nor a stay, nor a help; still less can it give you a friend."

Oh for a friend who understands friendship! This has been the theme of poets in all ages. I will not appeal to the glorious witness borne to this by heathen poets; let me rather quote from Christian literature, which will supply us with some admirable illustrations.

" Happy is he who has found a true friend ! he has found a treasure."

" A friend is the strength of life, and the strength of immortality."

And Saint Augustine exclaims :

" What is there more valuable, what sweeter and rarer, what more sought after and yet harder to find, than a true friend ?"

Such are the words he uses :

" What is sweeter and rarer than a true friend ?"

And then listen to that illustrious Frenchman, who, after spending thirty years in a foreign city, exclaimed :

" I lived there thirty years without finding a single friend."

Such had been the experience of his heart during his exile; he had not formed one affection on which he could rely.

But it is objected that independently of the supernatural order, it is possible to find friendship, and it is thus defined : community of intellect in the mind, and community of heart in affection.   It is further said :

"Friendship with our fellow-men may exist according to the natural order of human feeling; but God is so far off, so high above the world, how shall man reach unto God and live with Him in intimate communion?"

The day will come when on your deathbed you will exclaim :

"I ought to have learnt to live with God."

When the master of the household calls the outcasts of the city to his table ere he takes them by the hand, he bids them be transformed, and, laying aside their soiled garments, put on the nuptial robe. In like manner must the human soul be transformed ere it can ascend to God. The soul must lay aside her earthly garments to take part in the banquet of the friend whom God has given to her, to receive the Lord Jesus, Who is coming to her, and to take the hand which He holds out to her, when He asks for her love.

To whom, indeed, will you go if it be not to Jesus Christ? Where, save in Him, will you find your stay and your strength?

You drag along wearily in the dark valleys of the earth, like flowers which fade away for want of light and sunshine; your life wastes away, your soul languishes. Oh! come, come up upon the mountain, and behold this wonderful gospel scene.

One day three disciples of Jesus Christ, Peter, John, and James—zeal, purity, and martyrdom—ascend a steep mountain; they climb it laboriously, but when the top is reached they see before them a bright cloud; the cloud opens, and they behold a countenance shining with light, garments whiter than snow, and from the midst of a glory indescribable, a voice is heard saying—

"This is my beloved Son in whom I am well pleased; love Him! He is your ideal; He is love, purity, sacrifice."

And the disciples exclaimed:

"It is good for us to be here!"

Well then, my sisters, do you also take with you the spirit of zeal, of purity, of love, and of self-sacrifice; mount up to the summits of the Christian life; go forward until you reach that spring of cleansing water; then shall you see the shining cloud, and the cloud will open and the transfiguration of Jesus Christ will appear to you. He is your Head, your ideal, your stay, your Friend! Leave the earth ; go to Jesus Christ, and armed with purity, love, and self-sacrifice, you will be able to say :

"How good it is to be here."

The Obstacles to the Supernatural Life.

THE SPIRIT OF THE WORLD.

"We have received not the spirit of this world, but the spirit that is of God."—1 Corinthians ii. 12.

 HAVE already said, my sisters, that the whole secret of Christianity consists in the understanding and the ordering of life. I have further endeavoured to fill up this idea by adding that it is not enough to understand and to know how to rule over our lives. The understanding and the government of life might, to a certain degree, be apprehended even by a heathen, or by the natural man ; but we Christians have a further step to make; we must have the supernatural element, the life of grace—God within us. The supernatural is an uncreated strength; it is God dwelling and abiding in the soul.

This morning, I explained to you the way in which this supernatural life was carried on in our souls; how God had, as it were, taken up the ruins of our fallen nature, willing that out of these very ruins should be worked out our restoration. God has become our model, the ideal which we must imitate, the ideal which we meet with nowhere else; and that we can only find in Jesus Christ.

And this imitation of our Lord will call forth our noblest thoughts, our tenderest, purest, and deepest feelings, it will lead us onwards and upwards to a spirit of entire devotedness and generous self-sacrifice.

I have said also that in Jesus Christ we should find not only an ideal, but a stay, inasmuch as our weakness requires support; and a friend, because our hearts need affection to strengthen and ennoble them.

But although our Lord Jesus Christ should be, as we have seen, the Alpha and the Omega of the human soul, yet are there, both within and around us, many obstacles to the realization of this object. When speaking to you on the understanding and the government of life, I said that frivolity or sin was one of the chief obstacles to the attainment of perfection.

But what are really the obstacles to our putting on Jesus Christ ; to the establishment of the supernatural order in our souls ? They are, in the language of the church, three ; the spirit of the world, the spirit of self (the *I*), and the spirit of evil.

I purpose to examine these three obstacles one by one, and to show you both their weakness and their strength—their weakness, because you may conquer them ; their strength, because they may easily overcome your good resolutions. Let us this evening consider together what is meant by the spirit of the world.

What, then, is this spirit of the world ? What is its power ? The two thoughts which I wish especially to bring before you, are, that the world can never give you that which we saw this morning was given you by Jesus Christ ; that it can offer you neither a model, nor an ideal, nor a stay ; that the world is essentially opposed to the spirit of Christ, to Christian thought, and Christian practice ; that if you have the spirit of the world you cannot be good Christians. You may live in the world, and still be Christians, without increasing the number of your communions. The whole secret of the Christian life lies in the heart. Is your heart given to the world, or to Jesus Christ? You cannot serve two masters; and yet you generally strive to do so, and almost always it is Jesus Christ who has the second place. You hold out one hand to the lord of this world, the other to the Lord of heaven, and the world gets the best of it. My sisters, what I earnestly wish is to turn you away from this love of the world, and from its dangerous if not sinful compromises, and to show you that, next to your own selves, as we shall see to-morrow, your greatest enemy is the spirit of the world. She who is filled with the spirit of the world is, in truth, not a Christian, for this spirit is not that of Jesus Christ. You know with what ingenuity the world pleads its own cause, how it advocates it with the prestige of a seductive and insidious eloquence. The world attacks you in two ways. First it says, " People preach against the world. Who are they who do so? The priests. But what do they know about it?" Then it adds, " Is there any harm in the world? The world! it must exist; without it society would be impossible; and were there no organized society, the whole earth would be one vast cloister, peopled only with hermits. But it is not so; the world does exist."

This is true; but, as I said in a former retreat, the world is neither evil itself, nor is it the principle of evil, but still it is the atmosphere in which evil is propagated, the ambient air in which it floats, the power which gives to it a double strength. The world has a sort of external fascination which is always attractive, and therefore it is that in the world there is ever that danger of which Jesus Christ spoke when he said, "Love not the world, nor the things of the world."

Therefore St. Augustine, Bossuet, and all the great doctors of the Church, have anathematized the world.

In the world, there is your danger; and why? Because in it you will not find those three things, after which yearn alike your heart, your imagination, your feelings, and your whole being. You want an ideal; you are seeking it everywhere; you look for it in your dreams, in your homes, in your literature, in your sensational romances, in your theatrical representations. Everywhere, and in everything, you seek an ideal, and ever do you return with heart and mind alike void and unsatisfied, for nowhere is it to be found. Nowhere, as I have already said, but by the well of Jacob. In vain will you search for it in the tainted cisterns of this world. You will find it only in Him out of whom flows the well of living water, springing up unto everlasting life. Cast away your illusions, go to the well of Jacob, and you will hear these words, "*If thou knewest the gift of God!*"

Can we, indeed, find our ideal in the world? No, for there is in it neither beauty, nor goodness, nor heroism, and no great work can ever be done in the world without these three things. One of these three, apart from the others, may, indeed, exist. I mean beauty. The painter sees manifestations of beauty scattered here and there, and he gathers them together, and seeks to embody them on his canvas; but this plastic beauty is but the vision which his imagination has pursued, the creation of his own mind: it is an ideal.

Goodness! The unselfishness which seems to live but for others, which is ever giving, which is ever sacrificing itself. This, too, is an ideal, not to be found except in those who live above this world.

Heroism! In this vale of tears, we still find here and there some generous hearts, who seem to exist for the performance of great and noble deeds; but it is only on the wings of religion that they can attain to the sublime heights of heroism.

But do these three things exist in the world?

In the first place, there is no real beauty, such as appeared in our Lord Jesus Christ. He was the fairest among the children of men; His was true beauty, beauty which is of the intellect, and of the heart, and soul.

What does the world offer you? Nothing but illusion, nothing but frivolity, humiliation, and evil.

After all, what is the world? I refuse to draw a picture of it, to come down to the commonplace details of that petty mundane existence, whose horizon extends only from a toilette to a jewel, from a banquet to a fête, from the excitement of an evening party to the weariness of the following morning. What, then, is there in the world, but utter frivolity?

If you could but look into the heart of a thoroughly worldly woman (I am not now speaking of one who is constrained by the obligations of her position to go into the world), what would you find there? Can there be one single high aspiration, can there be any largeness of mind, in one whose whole life is absorbed by the preparations for some fête, some ball, in which she hopes to create a sensation, and whose highest aim is the invention of a new toilette? I ask, then, what is such a life, but one of utter frivolity—frivolity in dress, frivolity in conversation, frivolity in feeling? It is nothing else.

And yet, side by side with these frivolities, in spite of the prestige of fashion, and of the varnish of external fascination, there are things in the world which are to the last degree humiliating. There are criminal transactions, compromises of conscience, sins of the tongue, perhaps culpable weakness of heart. We find cowardice of heart, treason to the sacred rights of truth, to the virgin orthodoxy of the Church; and hence proceed, as I have said, compromises more or less humiliating, intellectual degradation, and a sort of moral timidity, supposing even such a career stop short of actual sin.   Remember, my sisters, that too often the path is slippery, and the descent rapid, of that road which leads from frivolity to humiliation, and from humiliation to ruin and to sin.

You think it easy to stand always upright in the world ; you trust to your virtue, to your temperament ; you have faith in your strength of will ; you shelter yourselves behind your personal dignity, and believe that it is sufficiently imposing to protect you.   But you are standing only upon a pedestal of clay, the clay crumbles beneath your feet, and you fall ; and your fall is ruin.

The world is not only the absence of the true ideal, the reunion of even frivolity ; it has also at its command its subtle reasonings, its lines of demarcation, its ready excuses, perhaps even its falsehoods and its sham virtues wherewith to hide its poverty.   I have said that the world has its lines of demarcation.   In fact, every one who goes into the world says to himself, " Thus far will I go, and no farther ;" they trace out limits to themselves, and say, " My passions shall not go beyond this point ; the stream may overflow, but I can stem its course." Oh, folly of the youthful heart ! nay, even, it may be, of that of riper years ! Look at the barriers which it has raised, both to the right hand and to the left, and deemed so sure ! A drop of water makes an opening, the torrent sweeps everything down before it, and there is nothing left but destruction and devastation.

Such is the world ; we build up barriers for ourselves, but they are carried away again. There is but one strong enduring barrier, and that is the spirit of earnest faith ; it is the heart full of the love of Jesus Christ ; it is the lofty nobleness of duty. Without these you cannot avoid evil. You may, perhaps, escape external evil, but there will still be the ravages of sin in the innermost heart and conscience. And is not this misery ?

Oh, the emptiness, the frivolity of the worldly heart—a heart whose aim should be eternity, a soul which should, if I may so express it, be a chalice filled with the Spirit of God, a chalice out of which to drink fully of eternity. Oh, how can such souls give themselves up to the intoxication of vanity and luxury? Are not such things unutterably sad?

And nothing can move such a heart. Not the fear of a husband who points to a tottering fortune; nor pain, nor sorrow, nor apprehension of remorse, nor even the sight of a child just growing up, already perhaps coveting the vain and sinful successes of her mother. Oh, frivolous soul, how great is thy ruin!

And there is something sadder still. In the world the soul may be said to be turned into a theatre, for the soul of a Christian woman, who cares only for the vain success and pomps of the earth, is nothing else than a theatre. The fear of sin, the word of God, the complaints of a husband, the good examples which a young girl requires on her entrance into life, the Blood of Jesus Christ, the mysteries of the Incarnation, and of redemption, the terrors of eternity, none of these things have power to move this earth-bound soul; it is carried here and there like a leaf before the wind, which at last falls to this earth, to be picked up by the first comer; and this first comer will always be the devil.

Thus, my sisters, you have seen that the world is not our true good—it cannot be your model. And if, instead of the picture I have myself drawn for you of the world, I had painted it according to your own individual appreciations, and your own intimate experience, you would have realized the truth of my words still more vividly and sharply.

And, next, does the world offer you a stay? There are three occasions on which the soul needs strength and support. First, in the time of temptation, in moments of hesitation, struggle, uncertainty, when she stands face to face with a grievous peril, and is on the verge of falling. Secondly, the soul needs a stay which shall strengthen her for duty, when that duty is before her, hard, painful, monotonous, perhaps intolerable. Again, the soul requires a stay in the hour of sorrow, when the heart is bleeding, and tears, bitter and scalding, gather in the eyes.

Is the world a stay in temptation ? Nay, indeed ! The world removes the barriers which might arrest you ; it opens its arms to you, sows flowers along your path, veils instead of revealing the abyss before you. Far from offering you a support against temptation, the world is itself a living temptation, subtle and treacherous.

Does the world help you in the fulfilment of duty? Duty, duty would teach you not to make so much display in your attire; not to wear on your heads the bread of the poor, not to put—I was going to say upon your shoulders—but on them you wear little enough! It would teach you not to carry upon your fingers, upon your arms, that which might perhaps be the support of a church, or furnish the sacred vessels to the poor missioner.

Does the world afford you a stay in duty when you leave your home, and go away in all your splendour and light-heartedness into the whirl of society, abandoning the care of your child to the hands of a hireling? The child grows up, and looks for the tenderness of a mother's heart; but the heart of the woman of the world is cold, and she forgets that she is a mother. Alas! the time will come when she will bitterly rue the hours once wasted in vanity and pleasure.

Will the world be your stay in the day of sorrow? Does the world go to the house of mourning? No, it turns away. Ah! I know full well that the world has its own modes of comfort, its sympathizing words, its graceful and pleasant courtesies. A man of the world, whose life had been spent in the turmoil of large capitals, once said to me:

"Nothing is stranger than our Paris life. We hear that some one is dead; we meet the son or the brother of the departed; we go up to him, shake his hand, and say: 'You have lost your father, your brother, what a misfortune!' Then we talk of the news of the day, of the papers, the races, of some party of pleasure, of other things. We shake hands again and part."

This is something like what happens on board ship, when some one dies; the body is cast into the sea, and the ship goes on its way.

The world, my sisters, will give you a few sentimental tears for a moment; but it will never be your stay in the hour of sorrow. I repeat it—the world is neither an ideal, nor is it a stay. Is the world a friend? does the world care for you? Yes; it does sometimes care for you, as it cares for a musical instrument, for a drawing-room flower, for a passing ornament, which sheds lustre on its entertainments, a unit increasing its crowd. Once more, the world cares for you, because you adorn it with your charms; when these charms are a little faded it delights in scorning and rejecting you. Has the world any heart? Is it not full of cruelty and hypocrisy? The world has taken hold of innocent hearts, crushed out with sinful hands their purity, and having done this, casts them away as dead bones, fit only for the charnel-house. All that the world requires are whitened sepulchres. When once vice shows itself in all its hideous reality, and becomes public, the world turns scornfully away; it holds out no pitying hand; it has no mercy. In that one grand incomparable scene of the Gospel we have the most vivid picture of Christianity and of the world. Look at that poor woman, guilty, according to the Jewish law. The world is the Pharisee; he asks but for one thing—let the sinner be stoned: let this poor fallen woman suffer yet more crushing humiliation; let her sink under her misery and her desolation. But Jesus draws near; He consents to be the Stay, the Friend of this soul, forsaken by all the world. And then, to those around her, He launches forth these words:

" Let him among you, who is without sin cast the first stone at her"—" *Qui sine peccato est vestrum, primus in illam lapidem mittat.*"

The Gospel adds that they all went away, beginning by the oldest.

When a poor woman has fallen, the world, if it knows it, points the finger of scorn at her; she meets with nothing but condemnation, reproaches, and opprobrium.   Jesus Christ alone comes near to this soul, and says to it :

" The world has condemned thee because thou hast sinned, but I will not condemn thee ; I will raise thee up again."

Christ absolves and blesses this soul ; He is the sole Stay—the true Friend of the fallen—of those whom the world has bruised and humbled ; He is the last Friend of those whom the world hates ; for the world does not and cannot love.

It is a fact, then, that in the world there exists for us neither a true ideal, nor a friend, nor a stay.

My sisters, let me speak plainly to you. Are not many amongst you essentially opposed to the Spirit of Jesus Christ ?   That which seems strange to us, priests, is to hear it said :

" Why all this condemnation ? Are not the words of the Gospel exaggerated ? Does not the preacher still further enhance their meaning in the high-flown language of the pulpit ?"

This is, indeed, to defend the world; but it is defending it without an adequate knowledge of the cause of its condemnation. The world stands condemned, because, beyond anything else, it saps the very foundation of Christian principles, Christian morality, and Christian virtue. For, in very truth, Christianity is based upon three supreme facts: Bethlehem, or poverty ; Nazareth, or work ; Calvary, or suffering.

These, my sisters, are the three fundamental corner-stones of Christianity.

You may make to yourselves according to your own fancy, your own caprice, another Christianity, enfeebled, enervated ; but it will no longer be the Christianity of our Lord Jesus. In our day everything is called Christianity (to use the words of Bossuet), everything, save only the Christianity of Jesus Christ.

The fundamental ideas of Christianity, I repeat it, are Bethlehem, Nazareth, and Calvary. You cannot alter it, God has bowed the heavens, He has come down, and has laid these three as the fundamental basis of our faith : the manger, the workshop, and the cross—poverty, work, and suffering. Poverty ! suffering ! what has the world to do with these ideas ? Does it even understand them ? Does it care for them ? Is it not true that in these days the necessity of growing rich has taken the place of the idea of poverty.

Who cares for poverty, when in our own days a poor man whose daily bread depended on the alms given him by the roadside, was exalted by the Sovereign Pontiff, until the very rags which covered him became, as it were, his robe of glory ? When our nineteenth century, infatuated as it is by its modern naturalism, was expected to admire in this beggar the impersonification of purity and simplicity of soul, then the Christian world smiled and could not understand it ; and why ? Because the world has invaded Christianity and thoroughly permeated it.

Modern society knows but one need, it has but one desire, one craving, one aim ; for its whole current gravitates round the golden calf, the passion for money gains ground everywhere ; money is coined out of everything, as it was in the days of ancient Judaism. Provided only that certain meshes of the law are avoided, no one cares for either society or conscience; the multitude rushes on headlong in the race after wealth. The idea of poverty has vanished. And work! In what esteem does the world hold work? What, work! Stain those white delicate hands!—that is left to the poor!

And many is the Christian woman, exalted in fortune, birth, nobility, and power, and filling a high place in this world, who feels herself tempted to say with the nobleman of ancient days:

"Surely God will think twice before damning one of my race!"

But will God indeed think twice before damning that high-born wealthy woman? No, for is she not of the same clay as that poor woman who labours from sunrise to sunset, and often too from sunset to early dawn, in order to earn for her children their scant and bitter bread? Who would believe that an age which proclaims with pompous phrases the glory of equality should draw distinctions such as these! You are the favoured of fortune, it says, you were not born to work!

Beware, my sisters; this worldly principle is spreading fatally, and if your lives are devoted to idleness (I know not why I bring together these two words), it is because you have not the spirit of Christianity.

And the idea of suffering! We shrink from every sort of constraint or annoyance; the whole spirit of the age is antagonistic to it. The laws of the Church, in spite of the numberless dispensations which she grants, will soon be little more than a tradition of bygone ages, an old curiosity, fit only for a museum of antiquities. Our Christianity must be no constraint to us.

And yet, my sisters, there is a dominion, far more despotic, more constraining; I mean the world. Were I to draw a parallel between the spirit of the world and the spirit of Christianity, you would see that the real tyranny is that of the world.

The world, remember, is the destroyer of the spirit of Christianity. Go into our large towns, it is to these especially that I allude; is it only the preaching of error with which the world contents itself? Does it not also with unblushing audacity, presume to sit in judgment upon the doctrines of the Church?

The words of the Sovereign Pontiff, are they not received with a smile which is responded to from every quarter of the globe? Is it not the same with the words of your priests, and your bishops, how are they received? How are they estimated?

Some particular book, it may be a pamphlet, a novel, is circulated in your drawing-rooms, and from these you form your judgment of Christianity; one might almost suppose that it was the object of the age to decoy the Church into some alliance with the vanity and interests of the world so as more surely to compass her ruin.

Again, in what esteem do men now hold the Sacraments of Penance and of the Eucharist! How low our Christian standard has fallen. And after nineteen centuries of Christianity we look in vain for Christian society, for Christian homes, or even for Christian life. I have sometimes asked myself whether, if some heathen were suddenly brought into one of our great European cities, and turning to a priest were to inquire where he could see

Christianity, the priest could point to anything except individual Christianity.

Vain would it be to seek for social Christianity in the fashionable world ; we must go to the humbler classes where the domestic hearth is still sheltered by Christian principles. Nowhere else are they to be found, and when we see how well the world knows how to defend its frivolity and its vanity, we may well take up the words of a great orator when speaking of the fewness of the elect :

" What remains then for Thee, O my God ?"

The world has no thought for God ; on the contrary, the spirit of the world tends to enfeeble Christianity, because, as I have said, the spirit of the world is the antipodes to the spirit of Christianity, and what of Christian observances ! On Sundays you vouchsafe to God the favour of your presence at a low Mass ! You come with hurried devotion to exhibit even in church the splendours of your position. During the week, you kneel perhaps, for one half hour before the altar, and our Lord may think Himself honoured and you expect His blessing.

And fasting, self-discipline, what do you know of

these? Do you carry out the law of labour? Let us see how your day is spent! You do not leave your bed till the sun is already high in the heavens. Your morning is often begun by harsh words to those around you, domestic quarrels ensue; wearied at heart, you go into society in the hope of forgetting your annoyances; the evening comes, and you have no thought but for the world and its admiration. Such is your life!

Now, I ask you, my sisters, is this the life of a Christian woman? I implore you to think of it seriously and to question your own hearts. You, who have sisters or daughters, could you be satisfied that their hearts should be thus empty and careless in the sight of God?

In our days the strictness of Christian life is in fact destroyed and done away with. I know, indeed, that in some places, as at Lyons for instance, the grand traditions of Christianity are still preserved; but on every side breaches are being made, you are destroying not only the ancient fortifications of the town, but, if I may so say, the fortifications of your own souls. And those venerable traditions of antiquity, how do we see them fall

6

beneath the ironical sneer, and the insidious attacks of your journalists and modern historians ! The clamorous echo of their words reaches even to the foot of our mountains.

In our Protestant city of Geneva, which has retained a Puritanism, exaggerated it is true, but possessing still, together with its strict sense of duty, the feeling of a Christianity, which although mutilated, still preserves a certain grandeur and majestic severity which we cannot ignore—in this city even, I say, we hear the vibrations of your worldly literature. Most true it is that modern society is no longer Christian ! . . . . Persons whose very degradation is the cause of their notoriety are openly discussed and admired; sometimes even you go so far as to copy the language, the habits, the customs of their ignoble lives. Take care; your models will at last, in their turn, force their way into your drawing-rooms, and claim their share of your enjoyments and of your position.

My sisters, remember that you are the guardians of Christianity, the defenders of its bulwarks. If you suffer these bulwarks to be overthrown, if you lend yourselves to their destruction, it is at the price of your own honour; your dignity, your influence, your power, come to you solely through Christianity, for it alone teaches the reverence, the respect due to women; from the moment you once cast off the sacred veil of its protection, from that hour, I say, the days of paganism will return; you will be but a plaything, a toy in the hands of man, to be broken and dishonoured at his will, and cast off when he is weary of you.

Such, my sisters, are the great lessons, the true teaching of Christian faith; you must understand and comprehend them. I am not exaggerating; I am but trying to throw myself into the spirit of the age, into the depths of the human heart, hence to deduct some practical conclusions and advice. Whilst I speak I invoke the gentle memory of St. Francis of Sales, in whose great and noble soul no exaggeration could find place. If, then, what I have said be true, if the world cannot be for you either an ideal, a stay, or a friend, if it be, in fact, the destroyer of Christian principle, ought you to mix in it?

Yes, for legitimate reasons oblige you to do so. First, there are duties of position, and these duties are imperative.

God has organized society; He has created the social hierarchy; there must therefore be the possibility of good and innocent society, and such society may be yours if you will but take your part in it with true, honest, Christian hearts.

Your influence may be the leaven which will Christianize society. It may therefore be a positive duty to your families, to your position, and to your husbands, to go out into the world.

And yet when we listen to your husbands—it is true that they may exaggerate—they complain of your overweening love of luxury, of your extravagance in dress, of the whirl of gaiety which has its fascination equally for them, but for which their dislike to restraint keeps them away, for in these days we hate the restraint which the world requires of us; there is no slavery like that of the world. We hear of fortunes crippled by your love of ostentation, by your lavish expenditure; we hear of your reckless exposure of health in the pursuit of pleasure, nay, that you do not hesitate to risk your very lives rather than forego the excitement and amusement of a single evening.

Whatever truth there may be in these reports

which reach us from the world, this much is certain; that by such conduct you ruin, if not your health, at least your fortune, your children's future. The powers of your mind are wasted on vanity and trifles, your heart and affections are frittered away, holy inspirations neglected; the life of God within you is destroyed. Such are the points I would beg of you to think over.

Go, therefore, into the world, if your position demands it of you, or in compliance with the legitimate wishes of your husbands, and for the furtherance of the future interest of your families; go into it even for the sake of innocent recreation; God allows this. There may be even circumstances when this is a positive duty; only take with you a spirit of faith.

It is a woman who has written these remarkable words:

"It is not every woman who can leave the world, but every woman can conquer it."

. Go into the world, my sisters, but go there with a true knowledge of it; remembering that behind its brilliant feasts it hides secret temptations and passions, and that the fell serpent of vice is con-

cealed beneath the flowers on which you tread.
Go into it full of the love of duty, not with hearts
weakly ready to give expression to the vexations
and the trials of your domestic hearths; do not
seek there a comforter who can understand you;
who, beneath your diamonds and your flowers, will
see your secret tears.

You are too ready to believe in sympathy, to
make confidences. A woman does not hide her
tears, and then she imagines herself to be understood. She is pitied, flattered, encouraged.

Every young man of twenty has now his sentimental phrases at command! And the woman,
who would laugh at the friend who came to her
with stories of her domestic grievances, believes
in such sympathy for herself just as Eve believed in
the serpent. Women are all daughters of our first
mother; they trust too little in God, and too much
in the serpent! Each one imagines herself to
be an exception; she thinks that she is especially
understood, that she has a peculiar individuality;
and she prides herself upon it.

Thus is the seed sown for future misery. The
day must come when the heart awakes to the con-

sciousness of its own emptiness.   Silence and darkness gather round it; remorse sets in; the veil falls from her eyes; the delicate bloom of a woman's fair fame is touched, and she is forsaken by all.   Then, in this hour of her desolation, her eyes are opened, and she sees herself as she is— the whited sepulchre of which our Lord speaks.

Think of these things, my sisters.   Go into the world with your hearts full of the love of God, of the love of duty, of the love of your children, giving due and sufficient care to your outward appearance, but ever remembering that modesty is a Christian woman's best ornament.   Happy the Christian mother who, before she goes into the world, kneels down to pray for her child, invokes its guardian angel, and making the sign of the Cross as she bends over its cradle, only leaves it that she may for a few moments give to her friends the comfort of her presence and her sympathy.

She does not turn night into day, but returns early to her home, happy in the consciousness of having done her duty.   Her spirit has not been ruffled by the sight of diamonds finer than her own; by smiles not intended for her; she has not writhed under the torture of that jealousy which poisons the life of so many women; no wounded feelings disturb or harass her on her return home.

The queens of society—I will not give them the name applied to them, that belongs to the Queen of the Desert—the queens of society believe in their own triumphs; but in their dreams by night, or rather by day, for night is not their time for sleep; they see themselves crushed and vanquished by a rival; they perceive only the smiles and the applause which has not been for them, they are unhappy, and their life is miserable.

And this shows you, my sisters, that if you are obliged to mix in the world you must do so in a Christian spirit. And be assured that society may be made Christian, that society is chiefly what women make it by their own imagination, their own tongues, and their own conduct.

Let me illustrate my meaning. Imagine yourselves on one of those iron roads which are the annihilation of space. A few drops of water which the action of fire has turned into steam, have sufficed to set in motion the powerful engine which is hurrying you along, and distance is now but a word.

Well, my sisters, in the onward march of Christian society—on the railway of the world—woman is that drop of water, that magnetic influence which, vivified and purified by the fire of the Holy Spirit, has power to set the social train in motion. Impelled by her, it hastens safely along the line of progress, and advances steadily towards its eternal destiny.

But if, instead of being this drop of water of heavenly grace, woman, on the contrary, becomes a stumbling-block, then we have dreadful catastrophes, fearful shocks, explosions, ruins; whole lives are destroyed.

The misery worked by the vanity, the petty coquetry of a woman of the world, the hearts she has broken, the souls she has ruined, the maledictions she has drawn down upon herself, she may not herself yet know; but in the day when all shall be made manifest, when the veils of earth shall be torn asunder, then shall the devastation she has worked rise up against her on her right hand and on her left, curses will be poured out upon her, the condemnation of the whole world will be upon her.

Let me entreat you, my dear sisters, to reflect seriously upon what I have said ; do not imagine it to be exaggerated. Consider my words in the clear light of life and in the yet clearer light of death.

Receive the blessing of Jesus Christ, which giveth more joy than all the false promises of the world.

The Spirit of Egotism.

"If any man will follow Me, let him deny himself."— Mark viii. 34.

Y sisters, the birth and development of the supernatural life should be the end and aim of our existence. But the soul can only attain to the fulness of this supernatural life, by the observance of the laws traced out for us by our Lord. Now these laws are hard, and we find within ourselves many obstacles toward their fulfilment. The first obstacle is our earthly spirit; the spirit of passion, which burns like a consuming fire; the spirit of illusion, which darkens the clear-sightedness of our intelligence; in a word, the spirit of the world.

I endeavoured yesterday to make you understand what the world really is, rather, I should say, to show you what is its spirit. I told you that you would find in it neither the stay which you need, nor the ideal which you seek.

The world cannot give you a stay, for it cannot give you love. There is no heart in the world, there is only passion. I say again, this evening, what I have often said before, that passion is no more affection than tyranny is government, or force power. There is the same difference between passion and affection as between brutal despotism and temperate government. Passion and despotism are selfish. The world is made of selfishness, taking everything and giving nothing. It succeeds in occupying and absorbing your minds with its frivolities and its trifles, but it deserts you in the hour of duty, in the hour of danger, in the hour of temptation, still more in the hour of sorrow, for the world is heartless.

You cannot find your ideal in the world, for the true Ideal is Jesus Christ, it is Christianity.

Now the world is opposed to Christianity, which can never flourish in its bosom. Christianity is a plant brought down from heaven; it is an exotic, fragile, delicate. How, then, should it live in so inclement a climate, in a temperature so harsh and ungenial ?

Christianity is built up upon poverty, labour, and sorrow. The world, on the contrary, lives but for gain, for show, for self-indulgence, and for idleness. It holds in abhorrence labour, suffering, and want, and looks down on Christianity with contempt and neglect. The world, therefore, cannot be the home of the ideal; and here we have the first obstacle to the supernatural life !

Yet have we seen that there are certain positions, certain obligations, certain lawful amusements, which may give you a right, nay, even which may make it your duty to go into the world. But, my sisters, you must do this warily, remembering that you are treading on dangerous ground.

You must go there, not in search of excitement, but for the sake of doing good ; not in quest of that which perhaps may be wanting in your home life, but that you may come to the rescue of those who are in peril, that you may carry comfort to the broken-hearted.

You must go into the world to fulfil a duty, to carry out a mission, an apostolate.

The second obstacle to the supernatural life is one of which I wish to speak to you this morning as simply and as familiarly as possible, in the hope of bringing before you some practical appreciation which may benefit your souls. And this obstacle you will find, my sisters, is, next to the world, in yourselves; your own selves; your own inmost being.

Nothing is so difficult as, through self, to rise up to God. Self, then, is our great obstacle. Therefore is it that there are those (whose heroism is not always understood) who thirst for God, who, if I may so say, are home-sick for heaven; who, before knowing the world, already feel a sad and ineffable weariness of life; and who, like the eagle, take their flight and soar high above the dust of this earth. To no created being has their love been given, their aspirations have risen higher, and their Spouse, the Chosen One of their heart, is none but God Himself! Their one aim in life is to destroy " self;" first, by tearing asunder whatever bonds may bind them to the earth; then by offering up upon the altar of purity and poverty all that is of this world, content to possess nothing, not even the grain of sand on which they tread, not even their own bodies which they have immolated ; yes, such as these may wing their flight to the supernal heights ; they have renounced self.

And now, my sisters, let me try to explain to you in what consist the chief perils of this " self," and what are the best means we can employ in endeavouring to renounce it. I would show you the obstacles which " self " offers to our sanctification, and how we may in time learn to overcome it, casting it like a grain of incense into the censer of praise which bears the homage of our souls even unto the throne of God.

My sisters, there is a deep mystery here below— a mystery, not greater, indeed, but as great, perhaps, as the inscrutable mysteries of faith. This impenetrable mystery, which in vain we try to solve, is the mystery of the human heart, the mystery of the heart of each one of you. It is the terrible struggle ; the strong impulses for good, and yet the lax indifference ; the mixture of heroism and of weakness, the infirmities which humble us to the dust, and yet the yearning to rise above them ; the proneness to fall under the first trivial temptation, and yet the courage, the devotedness reaching even to martyrdom; all this it is which make up that strange contradiction—the heart of man.

And how is this? Alas, it is because we are like a broken harmony, a harp of which some strings are cracked and broken, and whose music is but a discord. God created us, originally, to ascend to Him; but we have succumbed to the fascination of our own hearts, and the heavy weight of self-love chains us down to earth.

We are, so to say, in our present existence, pulled two ways. In the world all things oppress us, and weigh us down—business, cares, toil, anxiety—and the life of man is a life torn in two between the claims of heaven and the attractions of earth. It is a fight between God and man; a battle all the more agonizing, that in it, every way, the heart must bleed, wounded alike whether it be given to God or man.

There is a great deed for us to do, the mastery to be won over self. In the original divine scheme man was created for the exercise of two distinct powers: the power of joy or happiness, and the power of sovereignty. We are essentially created for happiness as well as for sovereignty; we are to be happy, and we are to rule. Holy Writ teaches us that when the reconstruction of the divine scheme shall be accomplished, these two faculties shall be restored in all their fulness to us in heaven; then we shall be happy, and we shall reign. It is said that the apostles shall sit upon thrones judging all the nations of the earth.

When God placed man upon the earth, He caused every living thing to pass before him. He showed him the herb of the field and the stars of heaven, and said, " All these things are thine, thou shalt have rule over them."

God placed woman by the side of man. She was to be united to man, and subject to him.

Then came a day of rupture. Woman desired to command. She employed seduction. But God manifested His anger; He said, "Woman shall submit; she shall conceive in sorrow; she shall bow her head in obedience." And since then it has been her constant aim to re-establish her sovereignty, to lay hold again of the sceptre which has fallen from her; so that, as man lives but for ambition, so does woman live but for dominion.

Unable to rule by strength, woman rules by her weakness and by her art. She endeavours to regain her power, not by any open attack, but by dexterous manœuvres; she does not erect barricades and proclaim a revolt, but prepares a subterranean mine, of which the explosion shall destroy the throne of him who rules over her and permit her to resume the sceptre of government.

My sisters, the love of power is strong within you; it is, in fact, the paramount desire of your heart. Well, this love of power is but the love of self, the exaggeration of your own individuality. You wish to command those around you. For what woman has not aspired to rule, were it but over the mind? what woman has not cherished the dream of reigning supreme in one heart? And if she has obtained this, is she not proud of her power? And beholding this heart, this little world at her feet, does she not say, with Cæsar, that she prefers being first in a village to second in Rome? Yes, she prefers sometimes being first in a heart debased and vile, a heart which has already yielded allegiance to many such capricious sovereignties, rather than content herself with sharing with a child or a mother the pure, calm affection of her husband. I know not what wretched infatuation takes hold of such a woman; she is possessed by the craving for power and for dominion. And this dominion she tries to obtain by finesse and address, using the many means of shining, and especially of pleasing, which are at her command.

For these, my sisters, are your weapons, this the strategy of all your warfare. You are coquettes from your birth. Were I not in this sanctuary, I might venture upon an illustration—rather far-fetched, you might think, perhaps. We have heard it said that at your very birth your first movement is to put your hand to your forehead to arrange your hair! And so the instinct of vanity is born with you and grows up with you; you find in it your sole strength and power, your one desire is to please and to shine.

Now, my sisters, all this is simply pride, vanity, an exaggerated estimate of your own personality, the " *I* " claiming to reign supreme. Now, as Jesus also claims to reign within you, and as He cannot accept your self-rule—for He is the Sovereign Master, and will not consent to be placed on a level with self in your heart—it is a struggle between you and God. Oh, you want to be the idol of others, because you are the idol of your own selves; your mind is absorbed with your desire of pleasing, your thirst for admiration, your talent for fascination, so that the power of the grace of Jesus Christ and the sweetness of His divine tenderness can find no entrance into your souls.

Now what is the result, what the consequences of all this?

That from this self-love, this exaggeration of your own personality, result three great evils:

1st. Obscurity, darkness, error, or illusion, they are all one.

2nd. Discomposure of mind, or restlessness.

3rd. Weakness, or discouragement.

Indecision of mind, restlessness of heart, discouragement of the will, these are the three consequences of self-love—I will not say the consequences of pride, for, as an author of unhappy celebrity has said, there are few who are lofty enough for pride.

All minds, nearly, are more or less narrow, more

or less mean, for vanity is common enough; it is
the strongest current in the stream of life. Pride
would have more serious consequences than this
restlessness, uncertainty, and discouragement;
pride leads farther; it leads to cruelty, to intolerable tyranny; it tramples upon every obstacle, and
knows no pity; for the proud brook no opposition,
no hindrance, which shall check their course. But
the three chief results of vanity are these: restlessness of mind, or intellectual error; disquietude
of heart; and infirmity of will.

We see, then, that the first consequence of self-
love and of vanity is restlessness of mind, or intellectual error. You deceive yourselves about others;
you deceive yourselves about yourselves.

With a skill that is truly feminine, satanic even
at times, how you excel in the art of lowering
others and exalting yourselves! With what incredible penetration do you not perceive the faults of
those you dislike, and even of those you like! How
you watch, how you dissect them! What tact you
display in this! How clearly, in the light of some
antipathy which you have conceived, do you dis-
cern the faults and weaknesses of another, to whose

good qualities you are blind or indifferent! There is in every human heart an innate love of detraction, which makes us impatient of the praise given to others, and tempts us to efface some one letter of the inscription engraved on their monuments.

How different it is when you yourselves are concerned! And, after all, who can be said really to know himself! One of the most intelligent men of our time, in speaking to me about his own powers, attributed to them the very opposite character to that which they really possessed. It is often thus. The poet believes himself an orator; the orator affects to be a statesman; the stern believe themselves gentle, the gentle passionate—we are all great at self-deception.

We see ourselves through the mirror of our own self-love, and self-love is a glass which magnifies or diminishes; magnifying our good qualities, and diminishing our faults until we behold them only in miniature. Thus is it that we are perpetually liable to error and delusion.

The second result of self-love is disquietude of soul, and this is one of the great ills of humanity.

In the world, my sisters, you are full of disquietude. I do not know whether I said yesterday —I cannot always remember what thoughts I have actually put into words, but you will forgive me if I repeat myself—I do not know whether I said yesterday, that, in the world, a woman finds it harder to yield to evil than to give herself up to good ; for evil brings with it the necessity of concealment, the wearisome struggle for self-justification, the vain attempt at self-delusion. Such is her life !

In the world there is anxiety everywhere. Even the most delicate and sensitive consciences, the purest and best souls, are moved at times by a disquietude of heart, which is as the shrinking of an angel from evil, but which with them takes the form of tormenting scruples. Our poor heart is like a pool of troubled water; our thoughts, our joys, our triumphs, our struggles, alike torment us ; we tremble at the spectre of the past, at the trials of the present, at the uncertainty of the future. This fear is innate in every human heart, and this it is which caused St. Francis of Sales to exclaim, "Oh, my Father, there is always something in me which trembles and is not satisfied."

And this feeling never leaves us. We are for ever trembling, most of all when we build upon our self-love instead of building upon God, when we know not how to build upon that sure foundation of peace, that city of Jerusalem, of which the Holy Scriptures speak.

Self-love is always anxious and troubled, foreseeing grievous misfortunes under circumstances which a little courage and faith would overcome. Self-love is envious, and exaggerates to itself the success of others ; it dwells on its own sensitiveness, and is jealous of its own dignity. And the heart thus absorbed in self is for ever disturbed and restless, especially if we are living only for ourselves and for our own self-love.

The third effect of self-love is discouragement. And this, my sisters, is indeed a terrible consequence. We cannot deny that in our own day we see more weakness of character than ever.

Does this arise from our system of education, from the relaxation of home discipline, from our milk-and-water Christianity ? or is it that the holy energy of faith, the grand inspirations, and the convictions of grace have lost their power ? Any way, weakness of character is one of the features of the present age.

I will not comment on this movement, which is thus affecting all classes of society; but I ask, where do we now find vigour and strength of character? Of course, it may be said, "Who is strong as the Lord?" But may it not also be added, "Who is weak as man? a leaf shaken by a breath, a reed broken by the wind!" Who is weak as woman? Instead of the saying of Holy Writ, "Who shall find a valiant woman?"—"*Mulierem fortem quis inveniet?*"—may we not rather say, "Where shall we not find a weak woman?" Yes, you are weak, you are open to every passing impression, any trifle takes hold of your mind; you are weak through the nervous susceptibility of your senses, weak through the restlessness and terrors of your imagination. You are weak through the childish credulity of your hearts, which a few soft words or smiles can captivate; you are weak through the inequalities of your temper; you make generous resolutions, which you are all impatience to carry out, but you soon give way, and do not keep them. Again, you are weak in your moments of depression, and you suffer yourselves to be overcome by them. Weakness may, in fact, be traced throughout your whole life. During your early years, just after your First Communion, when everything seemed smooth to you, how strong did you then believe yourselves!   There was plenty of enthusiasm within you at fifteen or sixteen, and holiness and self-sacrifice seemed so easy that you imagined you had but to stretch out your hand to seize hold of and practise them.   But when experience had taught you many a painful lesson, when year by year you saw your illusions fade away and vanish, you were at last compelled to say to yourselves: "I made resolutions, but I always broke them. My life has been unfruitful. I have fallen again and again, and after each victory has come defeat." Life is one perpetual race through a labyrinth of difficulties; your existence is but a succession of weaknesses.   Then some day, when your self-love has been wounded, you suddenly exclaim, "There is no longer any hope of success for me. I believed myself to be something, and I find that I am nothing but a heap of ruins."

Like the man who sees the materials with which

he was laboriously building his house borne away by the tempest, so you feel yourselves powerless before your own nothingness. And then discouragement seizes upon you. You had built on your own self-love. You depended on yourselves; and nothing remains to you but melancholy, and disappointment, and hopelessness. In vain do you seek forgetfulness of your troubles in the intoxication of pleasure. You are a burthen to yourselves. That is the very essence of self-love. And as you have not the courage to lay your burthen at the feet of Jesus Christ, you take it into the world.

And the world mocks at your discomfiture; the world sees and recognizes it, but without giving you even what you so much desired, the satisfaction of pity for your self-love. Thus you remain, a burthen both to yourselves and to the world. Oh, the world is sharper than you, and its self-love is wiser than yours; for it knows the very hour in which it will desert, abandon, and betray you—and that hour has already struck. You may still believe in your own conquests, whilst the world is already sitting in judgment on your defeat and your disgrace!

This study of the human heart, and of our inner

self, might be prolonged indefinitely ; for the human heart is truly a labyrinth, of which the mazes are endless. We might almost compare it to the subterranean catacombs of ancient Rome, those vast excavations so celebrated in the early Christian ages, of which the dark paths could only be explored by the aid of a lamp.

In like manner, when the brightness of revelation and the light of faith are brought to bear on the human heart, we marvel at the web of intricacies and contradictions which is then revealed to us.

This study may last a lifetime ; and even then, at the hour of death, when the last gleams of light reveal the soul to itself, even then we may exclaim, " I am a mystery to myself."

I cannot but smile at the sceptic, who refuses to believe in the mysteries of faith ; as if he were not a mystery to himself. His heart, his soul, his very being, even as yours, my sisters, is all a mystery ; and a mystery so unfathomable, that only at that hour when death shall have destroyed our body, and brought us face to face with God and the judgment-seat of Jesus Christ, only then shall we see all things naked and uncovered.

What, then, is the way to overcome self, so that, instead of being an obstacle to the supernatural life, it shall rather become a means which shall help us to attain to it?

In order to do this, we must act in direct opposition to self-love. Self-love disguises you to yourselves, it disquiets and discourages you. The life of faith, the supernatural life, must teach you to know yourselves, to bear with yourselves, to overcome yourselves. These are the three conditions essential to interior peace. Then, my sisters, will life become to you light and strength and joy.

To know yourselves, my sisters. Ah! here is the great difficulty. Our Lord has given us two means of doing so, which, in fact, may be resolved into one:

It is a word from within, and a word from without; it is you yourselves looking at self, and God looking at you.

It is the action of this twofold insight, united together in the study of the deep and dark labyrinth of the human soul In one word, the only way to know yourselves, is to see yourselves, and to let yourselves be seen. It is sad to say so, but the truth is that, although you often look at yourselves, you seldom see yourselves. You look at your face, you study it, you notice every fresh wrinkle, you are skilful in seeking to hide and efface them; but the wrinkles of your soul, the stains of your conscience, all those things which are more or less questionable, do you ever look at them? Do you perform this act, so small and yet so essential, which we recommend to you so often? No; who practises self-examination, who scrutinizes their conscience? And so it has come to pass that we have but a surface Christianity; we might almost call it a Christianity for outward show. And yet self-examination is the most important thing in life. Priests are bound to it; and religious, in the solitude of their monastery, examine themselves twice daily—at midday on their predominant passion and their besetting sin, and again at night as to how they have fulfilled their duties or given way to their weaknesses. And you, my sisters, in the midst of a life full of agitation and turmoil, amid all the uncertainties and storms of the world, you never have the courage to kneel down, and to give if but three minutes to this all-important duty! and yet you can devote whole hours in decking out and embellishing this wretched habitation of clay, which the eternal Architect may perhaps destroy to-morrow—this body which so soon will be in its coffin!

The great business of life is to look into ourselves, but this requires both courage and strength. Ah! how well Jesus Christ knew the mysteries of the human heart! He knew that man would never look into himself if it were not commanded; if confession were not the rule. Outside the Catholic Church it is rare to find men who search their consciences. And yet some few have had the energy to do it.

Franklin, for instance, had the courage to condemn himself to write down daily upon a sheet of paper the faults which he had committed, and at the end of the week to cast up the account. A strong character might be capable of this, but you, my sisters, you cannot do it without the aid of confession, and even then before you present yourselves at the tribunal of penance, you cast but a rapid furtive glance of a few minutes over your conscience; you see nothing but the broad outline, and you go to confession without having discovered the dark points of your life and without having studied them.

Real self-knowledge is very rare; therefore you require the kind, friendly, affectionate, paternal glance of the physician who has the diagnosis of your soul, and who is able to reveal it to you. There is nothing greater than this Sacrament of Confession, which is like a bright light to the human soul.

Independently of confession there remains still something that might be done; it has often struck me whilst reflecting on the various means of christianizing the heart. I have said to myself:

" Would that in married life, husbands and wives could learn in a real spirit of self-devotion mutually to help each other in the discovery of their faults and failings, pointing them out lovingly the one to the other, instead of bringing them up as subjects of angry and bitter discussion. Would, in fact, that they could thus affectionately enlighten each other, so as to advance together in the task of self-examination."

I once saw an instance of this in a young married

couple. Theirs was a perfect union ; the husband and wife prayed, examined themselves together, confessed together. They made their self-examination in common ; they studied each other, and thus together strove to advance in holiness. How deep the union of heart, how deep the peace of conscience where such confidence exists ! Nothing is more attractive than an open and confiding heart which has nothing to conceal ; nothing is grander than a soul which reveals itself.

Learn then to show yourselves to yourselves, my sisters ; learn to accomplish this great work of self-knowledge by self-examination and confession. You will then have made the first step and acquired a new power ; you will know your enemy, and a known enemy is a vanquished enemy ; no danger is easier to destroy than a danger which is seen, and when you shall have acquired this self-knowledge you will no longer be to yourselves an obstacle in the way to the supernatural life.

Your second duty is to support yourselves. To support oneself! What a wonderful thought! Support! We make use of this word in speaking of things that are physical or material ! A wall is in danger of falling, we prop it up ; we give it a support, and thus prevent its ruin and its fall. To support oneself, to understand that we are but a ruin ! For this, we need the intelligent appreciation of our own infirmity, the acknowledgment that by reason of the primæval fall our nature has become a ruin. This fact once established it becomes easy to bear with ourselves.

But how hard it is to bear with oneself! how heavy the burthen ! When our Lord sent forth His apostles to conquer the world, He gave them the secret of power in the command :

" Possess your souls in peace."

That is to say, " Learn to bear with yourselves."

This is our Master's teaching.

And you who will not bear with yourselves, you expect others to bear with you ! or rather you almost flatter yourselves that they have nothing to bear with from you. And this is one of the great mistakes you make ; you imagine that you are obliged to bear with every one and that no one is obliged to bear with you. You think that it is you who have to endure everything ; the impatience and the ill-tempers of him who is the companion of your life ; the caprices of your children ; the faults of your servants ; the fickleness of your friends ; the various trials of your position. And all the while it is you who oblige others to endure your ungoverned nature, your impetuous temper, your too prominent personality ; you would like to bring every one to your own ideas, to bend every-thing to your own will.

You, who know not how to bear with yourselves, yet wish to rule over others ! The secret of Christian perfection, as all the saints, from the beginning of the world down to St. Francis of Sales, have again and again told us, is to know how to bear with oneself.

Learn also to overcome yourselves ; this is the means of annihilating self.

Self-conquest, self-renunciation. Do not shrink from this idea like those weak and timid souls to whom the word represents but an array of penances and austerities. No, self-renunciation is simply to renounce the humbling superfluities in which our nature indulges.

Look at that tree, that majestic oak, towering in

vigorous growth on the mountains. Its foliage gives shade, but on its wide-spreading branches parasitical plants are growing; take them away and the tree will be more vigorous still, and the leaves will expand yet more, and flourish more luxuriantly. And so it is with the soul: to renounce yourself is to renounce the parasitical plants of your life; to cast away whatever the devil and sin have brought into it; to mortify your senses in order to be able to govern and master them. You are not, for instance, to give up your imagination so as to destroy it; but so as to enable you to rule and direct it.

It is the same with your heart and its affections; we do not ask you to petrify and to stultify them, but merely to guide them that they may be in harmony with a truly Christian spirit. Your mind is not to be crushed and put in bondage, but it should be directed in such a manner that it may not be exposed to the caprices of your intellect. Neither do we call upon you to renounce happiness, for self-renunciation is happiness and joy; there alone is Jesus Christ to be found; self-renunciation is self-conquest, it is the putting aside of all that depresses and weighs down the soul, so that it may become like unto some pure vessel of gold, a fit dwelling-place for Jesus Christ, Who will then come and take possession of it, saying :

" My yoke is easy and My burthen light."

Thus, my sisters, will you learn the wonderful secret of a Christian life. To know yourselves, bear with yourselves, deny and overcome your-selves.

A great man once made his appearance in the world, a man who knew by experience all the struggles and the needs of an ardent and a passionate heart ; he knew, and had felt the desire for glory, the pining for affection, the craving to love and be loved, the longing for self-gratification and pleasure ; and when this man, when St. Augustine (for it is of him and his confessions that we are speaking), conquered at length by his mother's tears and by a voice from above, forsaking his life of self-indulgence and dissipation, recovered purity of heart and holiness of mind, there was ever on his lips one beautiful and incomparable prayer. After that hymn of joy and thanksgiving in which he said to God : " O beauty ever ancient, yet ever new, too late have I loved thee !" he made each day this prayer:

"My God, grant that I may know Thee and know myself!"

And this cry came from his very soul : "Grant that I may know myself, that I may know my infirmities, that I may govern my senses, that I may regulate my imagination, that I may rule my heart, that I may raise my mind, that I may infuse into my soul supernatural desires; grant that I may mistrust myself, my imagination and my passions. If I really know myself, I shall know the very essence of infirmity and misery. And if I know Thee, O my God, I shall know true beauty, true loveliness, true grandeur, the source and origin of all power and splendour."

May you then, my sisters, learn to know yourselves and to know God. And if, during this retreat, I can succeed in teaching you these two great secrets, I shall have taught you the two things most essential for obtaining peace and joy and holiness in life. I shall have taught you to know yourselves and to mistrust yourselves ; to know God and to trust in Him: and these are indeed two great secrets; for in ourselves there is naught but peril and sadness and misery; but in God is strength and joy and everlasting life.

The Tempter.

" Et accedens tentator dixit ei."—" And the tempter coming, spoke to Him."—St. Matthew, chap. iv.

 SPOKE to you this morning, my sisters, of the two great existing obstacles to the Supernatural Life, which prevent God's grace dwelling within the soul, Jesus taking possession of our consciences; we saw that these obstacles were: first, the world, and secondly, that love of self which brings with it delusions of the mind, disquietude of heart, and discouragement of the will.

But this is not all, my sisters. How numerous are the hindrances which are constantly impeding us; how are we encompassed on all sides by enemies who seem to press round and about us! And there is one enemy of whom no one thinks, especially in these days. I hesitate, almost, to mention him ; I mean, the devil, the tempter. For, the tempter exists, not only the visible tempter, whom you know, whom you have met, whom you find sometimes in your own homes, in the sufferings and the reminiscences of your own hearts ; but the tempter, whose presence is real, although it be invisible. Therefore is it that I have quoted these words: "And the tempter coming, spoke to Him."

No one can escape this universal law of holding converse with the tempter ; he has the power of speaking to every soul ; he draws near to every conscience, and he speaks to each. From the soul lost in the depths of the lowest grade of creation to the one placed on the uppermost heights of the social hierarchy, one and all must undergo the approach and the wiles of the tempter.

I would speak to you this evening, my sisters, about this great obstacle to the Supernatural Life. I have spoken about the spirit of the world and the spirit of egotism ; I am now going to speak to you about the evil spirit ; I ought courageously to say *the devil;* but I say the evil spirit on account of the over sensitiveness of the age we live in.

You are intelligent beings, my sisters; you are clever, or at least you believe yourselves to be so; well, then, confess honestly that you marvel that I should tell you so crudely this fact that "the devil exists."

Do you not rather look upon it as a legend, a tale of olden time? Is it not to you like some story of the Middle Ages, some tradition of the past, which you think ought almost to find its place in a museum?

No, my sisters, the tempter exists; the devil, Satan, exists, and neither your smiles, nor the denial of the world, nor incredulity, nor doubts, have power to destroy his existence, any more than the breath of a child would have power to blow down the walls which now surround us. It is certain that he exists; I will not do you the injustice to believe it necessary that this should be proved to you; you are too christian not to allow it, although your Christianity may sometimes be rather sugar and water.

In our days people would like a Christianity

without miracles, without grace, without the supernatural, without punishment, and without the devil;
they desire a comfortable Christianity; something
mild, sweet, soft, and agreeable, a Christianity suit-
able to the dreaminess of our nature, something
which shall embrace a certain element of seculari-
zation; a Christianity, in fact, weakened and cur-
tailed.

There is, however, a slight difficulty in this, and
it is that Christianity was made neither by you nor
me; neither by the Episcopacy nor by the Priesthood, neither by the Pope nor by the Church.
Christianity was made by God; if you complain
of it, as it is, you must ask God to alter it. We
dare not be faithless to our duty; from the Pope
down to the last of his priests, none dare whisper
in your ears pleasant words which might soothe
you, or which would feed and flatter your imagination and your heart; for they would be contrary to
truth. We can but say to you: "This is Christianity in its naked reality."

The devil exists; there is incontestable proof
of it in two pages of that Book which is the source
of all light. The first page of the Old Testament

opens with a conversation between the tempter and Eve in the terrestrial paradise. In one of the pages of the Gospel we see how the tempter approaches the Head of the human race, Jesus Christ. In order to deny the existence of the tempter, we should therefore be obliged to destroy the annals of the world.

There is no nation on the earth that has not believed in the existence of the evil spirit; some have even exaggerated this belief, and gone so far as to imagine that there is a good deity and a bad deity, who are perpetually waging war against each other here below.

Again, the existence of the tempter is proved by two phases in the history of mankind which are daily developing themselves more clearly.

Think of those terrible moments in life when every soul, even the best and the holiest, is exposed to temptations so violent as to be well-nigh overpowering! Then does the soul feel itself to be in a grasp which is not that of man; something stronger and more invincible than any human power. There is no child of sixteen who has not felt this revolt, this turmoil of the soul. Go and stand on the summit of a high rock, and look down into the abyss before you—your head swims, your sight is troubled, you are seized with giddiness, according to the common saying.

Well, there are times when conscience, looking down from the heights on which she sits enthroned, sees the abyss of temptation yawning before her, and feels the approaching whirlwind which shall envelop and overthrow the soul wherein she dwells. Surely then there is a power stronger than that of man ; there is an evil which is supernatural.

Another proof, still more convincing, of the existence of the evil spirit, of the devil, is to be seen in those dreadful crimes, in those fearful tragedies which occur from time to time in social life. Every now and then there comes an explosion, which betrays the depth of the evil that exists; then we are appalled, and say: "No! to such lengths of iniquity man alone would not go; it is beyond mere human wickedness."

Look at one of the " Little Sisters of the Poor," the impersonification of heroic self-devotion; she is often a person of high birth and of large fortune, who has had a luxurious home at her command. But the hour of sacrifice comes; and all is given up, and in the midst of her youth and strength she goes forth, it may be to some distant land, and submitting herself to the yoke of obedience, she envelops herself in a poor black cloak, and begs from door to door for the maintenance of the old men and women of whom she has become the servant and the friend, watching over them in their sickness, living upon their leavings and often receiving from them, for all return, complaints and murmurs and ingratitude; and for forty or fifty years, perhaps, she will carry on this heroic life; her name, her birth, will remain unknown to all; she may be in a non-Catholic country, or even in a Catholic one; she will be seen passing along in the street; but men will not understand her wonderful self-oblation; and they will heap abuse upon her, and will even dare to insult her!

Now, for the last nineteen centuries the Catholic Church has been this " Little Sister of the Poor." You do not know, my sisters, what an implacable hatred there is in the world, at the very core of humanity, against the Catholic Church, against that Church whose mouth opens but to bless, whose hands are ever stretched out to give bread to the poor, who is for ever pleading the cause of those who suffer, ever enlightening the souls that lie in darkness, ever drying the tears of those who weep. There exists, in fact, a spirit of the most inveterate hatred against the Catholic Church; and the desire to insult and calumniate and abuse her may be traced in innumerable publications, in books even with the most gorgeous bindings! Do you believe that man was created thus to hate and to abhor? I myself do not believe in man's power of hatred. Man has always a heart, and in every heart, even the most hardened, there still may be found some cord which will vibrate with feelings of affection and tenderness.

In order, therefore, that man should have arrived at such a pitch of hatred against the Catholic Church, he must assuredly be impelled by some supernatural and evil power. What is it which keeps up and sustains the self-devotedness of the Priesthood, of Missioners, of the " Little Sisters," of all religious communities under every name and form?   It is supernatural life, that source and mainspring of all the devotion, the self-abnegation, and the charity which we find in Christianity. Jesus Christ gives us the power to love! On the other hand, the devil, the tempter, by insinuating himself into the hearts of men, gives them the power to calumniate, to insult, and to hate.

Do not tell me, therefore, that the devil does not exist! These facts, these manifestations, prove it. When I see the sun's rays, I believe in that great luminary of the world. When I see the power and the malice of hatred, I believe in the devil, in the tempter, in the great enemy of mankind. And what is it, my sisters, which goes on between the tempter and man? It is a real drama. In the world you have often been at a play; you have sought therein excitement and emotion; your eyes have been filled with tears for artificial sorrows; your hearts have beat for fictitious woes! Well! between you and the tempter a drama takes place. A drama which opening in the terrestrial paradise is continued in the desert, when, as the Gospel tells us, the tempter dared to draw near to our Divine Master; and throughout the course of centuries has this drama been carried on. The devil comes, and with him comes temptation.

Remember, however, my sisters, that if there is great danger for us in being tempted, there is also great glory. In permitting us the use of our liberty, God has allowed us to be exposed to great danger, and yet it is also an incomparable privilege. Together with our existence, God has given us our free will in order that we may thus have the merit of trial, of temptation, and of conflict. Man only becomes strong through trial; the man who has never been tempted is weak. What can that man do who has never struggled? what can he know of himself? Trial is the secret of man's strength.

If the homage offered by creation to its Maker, were but that of the silent hills, the fragrant flowers, and the glorious sun; were there but the universe to sing the praises of God, it were but the homage of inanimate nature, not the homage of man freely tendered to his Creator. Man is free to love as he is also free to hate; he has freedom to render homage, or to refuse it. Thus has God willed it; only, together with this liberty of action, He has permitted the existence of the devil. The devil, therefore, draws near ; in what consists his art ? And first, what is the meaning of the word *devil.* In Latin *diabolus* means calumniator. In the primitive translations we find only the word *calumniator.* A calumniator means some one who conceals what is true, or one who gives out what is false for truth. The great art of the devil is to conceal what is evil, to gild over appearances, and to make them attractive. If you saw evil in its fearful reality, you could not love it, and you would never allow yourselves to be seduced by it. There is not one amongst you, however badly disposed, who would follow after evil were it seen as it really is. Evil must be disguised. For this reason it is that in our own language we so often say that there is a serpent beneath every flower. Something attractive or fascinating is required, a lovely flower, some sweet and intoxicating perfume ; when the tempter has designs on a soul he does not come openly with his face uncovered ; no, he comes with a mask, with deceptive ways ; thus is seduction concealed and dissimulated.

With Eve he enters into conversation. He appeals at first to her senses; and her senses are very impressionable, for her nature is quick and soon moved! He points out the fruit—she looks at it; she had never thought of it before; now she sees that it is pleasant to the eye, her senses are awakened, she gathers it. Then, how clever is the tempter! he begins a discussion with Eve, not at first denying anything, but simply suggesting an uncertainty, a simple doubt; he says: "*Why has God commanded you that you should not eat of this tree?*" He knows the reason full well; but it is his policy to make this subtle and perfidious question. And later on he adds: "*God doth know that in what day soever you shall eat thereof your eyes shall be opened and you shall be as gods, knowing good and evil.*"

Mark the progression: a look cast upon a seductive object, an insidious question, then a falsehood, then a fall. Such is the history of every temptation. In the world temptation appears under a threefold form; temptation of the senses, or concupiscence; temptation of the intellect, or pride; temptation of ambition, or of the will; whether it be ambition to possess the goods of this world, or ambition to possess a heart, it is always ambition.

Temptation often comes to you in this way.

A woman, we will say a married woman, is in her home; that home which ought to be her very paradise of delight; but alas, this paradise she seeks elsewhere. God chose her in the springtide of her young womanhood, and by His creative power gave her a soul destined to be united to that of another; by an eternal predestination He created them for each other, and foreordained their union; she the more sensitive, he the less disciplined, perhaps, but each destined to help forward the other in promoting the glory of God. But instead of thus carrying out the designs of her Creator, this woman consents to listen to the voice of the tempter; and he fills her mind with visions of other pleasures, other enjoyments; he places before her the fascinating attractions of the world, and then he says to her: "Why should you thus bury yourself at home? You are sad, why not accept the comfort and the sympathy of a heart that can understand you? I know that you are tied to a being thoroughly uncongenial to you;

you are misunderstood ; you are sacrificed to a man who is both coarse and stupid ; why not then listen to one who knows how to appreciate you, to one who loves and adores you......who asks but to die at your feet in the ecstasy of his devotion......?" And what more, my sisters, you know better than I, such like high-flown and romantic phrases, to which I ought hardly to allude—here—in presence of the Tabernacle.

Thus, however, does the tempter draw near to you, and soon you yield to the seduction. You allow it to sink into your hearts ; it reappears in your dreams ; you dwell upon it when you are awake ; when you are uneasy and discontented it comes to you as something pleasant, as a ray of sunshine in your life, as a consolation, a refreshment, an innocent friendship. You set yourselves a boundary, and say you will go no farther ! Alas ! you have parleyed with the tempter ; there was your first danger ; and from this parley, that is from the temptation to the fall, there is but a step, and that step is soon taken !

Eve fell ; and her fall was terrible. When the tempter addresses himself to a woman, he has on

his side the cleverest and the most insidious accomplices : her quick and impressionable nature,
her imagination so easily excited, so eager to
be fed.

Tell a woman that she is miserable, and misery
will appear before her with an appalling reality ;
promise her happiness, and a vision of untold joy
springs up before her.

Again, the devil takes as his accomplice our hearts
—our hearts which are so often sad, suffering, and
desponding ; for our hearts suffer ; it is the nature
of all hearts. We are not created for what is
perishable, for the things round about us, imperfect
as they ever are on one side or on another ; we are
created for the infinite, and as long as we do not
possess what is infinite, we shall possess but a drop
of troubled water.

Go forth in search of a brighter sun, a purer
sky, of keener affections, you will always end by
saying :

"The sun is dim, the sky is overcast, I am
wretched, my heart is void."

You might take the whole mass of creation, you
might press it in your hands, and, extracting its

very essence, drink it down at a single draught : still would not your heart be satisfied, because the world is finite, and your heart needs the infinite. Between your heart and the world there exists, if you will permit me an expression of every-day use, a "*mariage de convenance*," "*de raison*," that is to say, an alliance between people not suited to one another. You are suffering : your heart seems to require something different from what you have; you listen to the tempter, and your heart thus becomes the accomplice of the devil.

Besides the heart, the mind, the imagination, and the senses, the devil has, as his accomplices, your passions. By nature every woman is full of passion. You essentially want equilibrium, ballast ; in your life, in your whole organization, there is always something which is in excess; now passion is in excess. The devil, therefore, takes advantage of your passions. I do not say, indeed, that you must destroy these passions, but you must govern and wisely direct them; you must, as St. Theresa says, "Take hold of your heart and transform it ;" and we know how she "took hold of her heart ;" how she gave all its affections to God, and how

He, in return, rewarded her by an abundance of celestial sweetness.

We see, then, how the devil makes use of our passions; so clever is he that he appeals to every part of our nature. He does more, he induces you to commit a fault, and when it is done, when you have really fallen, when you come to see how your soul has offended God, when you feel that the purity of your conscience is sullied, when you have lost sight of the Divine Majesty, then, only, do you look at yourselves, and, like Eve, you see your misery, and you blush for it.

The first consequence of the fall is shame, or remorse. And happy is it for us that God has still left in the depths of the human soul the angel which we call remorse; for a time, indeed, he may sleep; but the hour comes when he will shake off his stupor, and come and knock at the door of our hearts.

Remorse, shame! sorrow for having fallen! Ah! happy will it be for you if this angel of remorse can wring from you tears of real repentance; not tears of offended pride, of mere sensibility, or of crushed and humiliated self-love; but tears such as St. Augustine shed, when he exclaimed: "What sweetness, O my God, is there in weeping!"

I have said that between temptation and the fall there is but one step, there is but one more from the fall to despair. Despair may follow on remorse; despair! that most terrible word in the whole human language; that word which is the very embodiment of all evil; that one feeling which the devil desires to infuse into mankind.

Thus Eve, flying before the voice of the Eternal and the angel's flaming sword from the earthly Paradise, entered upon the path, along which she was to find, lying in the dust, the lifeless body of her son; and then did despair seize hold of her, and she wept because of the innocent blood that had been shed.

The last resource of the tempter is despair, despair at having fallen. When the soul has fallen, when she has lost her innocence and her honour, when she has lost her God, then does she despair.

If it be a man of the world who has parleyed with the tempter, discussing with him important questions of doctrine or of Christianity, then his intellect becomes the prey of scepticism. How often have I come across men who had thus been ruined, minds who had lost their faith, and yet were seeking it, seeking it, however, in the pride of their intellect, instead of in the humility of faith, and by the blessed means of prayer. And souls such as these are ever ill at ease, and in their agony they exclaim:

"What is there beyond the grave, beyond death?"

This is death drawing nigh to an intellect which despairs, when it is not only the intellect, but conscience, which exclaims:

"I am tarnished, I have lost my baptismal innocence, I have crushed all that was noble and good in me, I have defiled myself."

Then this conscience, beholding so sad a picture of herself, is tempted to sit down beside the ruins of her lost virtue and, amidst the tears of her agony, to cry: "I despair!"

Despair is also the punishment reserved by God for those hearts who have abused their affections, and who are no longer capable of loving. The dead no longer hear the song of life. Some hearts

seem, as it were, to have " gone out." They despair ;
no longer able to love, all that remains to them is
a sort of cold selfishness, and, it may be, some
kind of animal passion. They are what we might
call petrified hearts, who seem to have been cast
down into the dust without more power to rise up
again than the bird, whose wing has been broken
by a ball, has power to extricate itself from the
mud of the road where it has fallen.

Despair, therefore, is the tempter's one great
resource. The tempter is the very impersonification
of despair. It is despair which makes hell. When,
after some sad fall, a soul, contemplating the
ruins of her former self, exclaims : " I despair !"
she has said all that is most terrible in the
language of humanity. Dante, that great Italian
poet, could find no inscription more appropriate,
more fitting, to place on the gates of his " Inferno "
than the words :

" Ye who enter here, leave behind you all hope !"

When St. Theresa was once questioned about
the devil, she gave an answer full of incomparable
beauty, revealing, at the same time, the angelic
tenderness of her own heart.

" The unfortunate one," she said, " he can no longer love !"

Despair destroys truth in the mind, faith in the conscience, and affection in the heart, and the tempter's one great aim in the world is to lead men to despair.

Does their hope no longer exist? I will tell you in a few words.

You are so accustomed, my sisters, to have related to you the great truths of Christianity, that they often come before you without making any impression. The scenes of the gospel are quite familiar to you; you have grown up with these stories of your childhood; they have been repeated to you both by your mothers and by your priests. And yet there is in the gospels one passage of which I must remind you; I alluded to it at the beginning of this meditation; it is when the devil approaches our Divine Master in the desert. The first phase of Christianity is the victory over temptation; the first phase of humanity was the victory of temptation.

Our Lord went into the desert. Observe this word " desert," my sisters. It is a grand thing to go sometimes into the desert ; I mean into retreat. You only go into the desert when you are tired of the world, or when the world is tired of you ; you only seek for solitude either when tired of your fellow-creatures, or when they are tired of you ; then do you feel the need of solitude. There are certain moments in your life when, like David, you exclaim : "O solitude! O solitude."

To be in solitude, in retreat, is to be above humanity.

Our Lord began the salvation of mankind by a retreat in the silence of the desert. For the sake of fortifying and strengthening the souls of men, He would not be exempt from temptation. He knew that His life was to serve as a model for mankind, and in order that mankind might not flinch before any obstacles, He chose to give an example of temptation really vanquished. And the devil approaches. I can understand that the devil should dare to approach if concealed by flowers, or that he should crawl along the ground, and address himself to a poor weak woman, although still encircled by her virgin innocence, and by all the grandeur of her primitive origin :

but that he should dare to speak to Eternal Beauty, to Eternal Truth! The greatest commentators of theological science have in vain tried to comprehend how the devil should have dared to approach God.

But if he did indeed draw nigh to Him, yet was it in a spirit of uncertainty. The devil has not infinite knowledge; he cannot see into futurity; he has, perhaps, suppositions which may be more politic and more cunning than those of this world; but he has no prophetic vision; he has sufficient insight to know how to attack and to tempt us, but he cannot conquer us, unless we consent.

Now the devil knew that the great mystery of the Incarnation was to transform the world; that it was to be the means of bringing into it such virtues as would wage war against the kingdom of hell.

Therefore it is that he approaches Jesus: he wishes to make sure that He is the Son of God; and he speaks to Him—he dares to speak to our Lord!—he says to Him:

"If Thou be the Son of God." He suggests a doubt, just as he had once said to Eve, " *Where-*

fore." He comes to Jesus with a doubt : "*If Thou be the Son of God, command that these stones be made bread.*"

Jesus had fasted forty days and forty nights, but He answers with simplicity, for falsehood is always conquered by simple and naked truth :

"*Not in bread alone does man live;*" that is to say, " Thou art trying to tempt Me through the senses because I am in want of food, because I am exhausted by fasting ; but," He adds, " man lives by every word that proceedeth from the mouth of God."

Then the devil is immediately vanquished.

But the tempter is not content with words; he dares to draw still nearer to Jesus, and he carries Him in his arms. And this is truly one of the most striking things ever permitted by God ; we marvel that it should have been allowed that His eternal Son, the Word made flesh, His own glory revealed to humanity, should have been taken by the devil, first on to the top of the temple ; then on to the summit of a mountain. The most sublime poetry, the grandest paintings, have failed in depicting this scene out of the temptation of Jesus Christ.

—the source of all beauty and of all peace—in contact with him who is the impersonification of hideousness and disorder.

After the temptation of the senses comes that of the intellect. The devil says to Jesus :

"*If Thou be the Son of God, cast Thyself down, for it is written that He has given His angels charge over Thee, and in their hands they shall bear Thee up.*"

This is the temptation of the intellect, of the reason—a temptation to rashness which disbelieves in danger. But the Master answers : "It is written, again, *Thou shalt not tempt the Lord thy God.*"

Then on the summit of the mountain comes the temptation of ambition. The devil shows Jesus the kingdoms of the world, and says to Him :

"*All these will I give Thee, if, falling down, Thou wilt adore me.*"

He demands adoration, and this is the last crowning act of his presumption. And yet it has been known that men have existed who have committed the frightful sin of worshipping the devil. Our Lord answers Satan :

"*It is written, The Lord thy God only shalt thou adore.*"

When the soul is weak she worships the devil; for how often in life, in the exaggerated language of passion, in the language of romances and of the drama, we find the words "*adoration*," "*adoring*." Have not created beings told you that they adored you? And this the veil behind which the devil hides himself, in order that creatures may be preferred before the Creator. Jesus answered:

"*The Lord thy God shalt thou adore, and Him only shalt thou serve.*"

The temptation was conquered by these words—Jesus was victorious. In order to overcome the devil, what is needed is to be simple, true, and straightforward.

But the surest way of overcoming temptation is to avoid it; to fly from it, not to encounter the danger. Believe me, there is always danger for you whenever you think there is danger; and you know it yourselves far better than your confessors do. There is always danger for you in any position which is in any way compromising, whether you are strong or weak; learn to keep out of the way of peril, and do not play with edged tools. Recollect what is written in Holy Writ, "Separate yourselves!"

It is by flying from danger, by keeping aloof from it, by not going near temptation, that you will be victorious.

And then, should you ever have the misfortune to give way, if you should fall, do not let your soul give way to despair. Despair ought to have no place in this life; its place is only on the threshold of eternity or of death. Even were your soul all that is most benighted, your conscience all that is most base, your heart all that is most vile, still would one great resource be left open to you. For the transformation of a soul, one glance from Almighty God suffices; one tear which, falling from our eyes, is seen by Him; for when God sees the soul through a tear, the soul recovers its beauty and its glory. Therefore, in order to escape despair, you have but to find the path of repentance; you have but to send forth a cry which shall reach to God, saying:

" Lord, have mercy on me, I am miserable, my soul is humbled."

The voice of the soul of man is very powerful with God.

If, on the contrary, you have not allowed yourselves to be overcome, if prayer has given you strength and saved you from falling, then shall you be full of joy. We are told that "*the desert was there, but angels approached it and it was no longer a desert.*"

The devil's great art consists in persuading you that if you will listen to him your life will no longer be overshadowed by darkness, that your heart will be free, your imagination no longer held in bondage, that you will no longer be fettered by penitential practices.

Not so, my sisters; if you can learn to overcome temptation, far from being in darkness, your life will be one of brightness and of light. How grand it is to see a soul which has triumphed over temptation! To her the gates of heaven are opened; she sees on either side the rejoicing angels and the Spirit of God Himself comes over her, filling her with a sweetness and a joy unknown, undreamt of. Go, then, with Jesus into the desert, and you will see whether the fulness of joy is not yours. But let the serpent allure you to make trial of the paradise of delight, and be sure that it will be your ruin. You must make your choice; the desert with Jesus, where you will find angels and joy, or the paradise of earthly delight with its flowers, and the serpent which is concealed beneath them ; and these flowers are thorns, remorse, too often despair.

You stand between Jesus and the tempter—between the flowers which fade and the angels who draw near ; leave, then, the flowers of this world, they are dead and fit but to be burned. Wing your flight above, soar higher and ever higher until you reach unto the angels, even unto God.

Life of Faith.

" The just shall live by faith."—St. Paul.

MY sisters, I have already said that if you are to have within you the supernatural life, it is necessary that you should not only understand and appreciate, govern and utilize, your existence, but also, and above all, that you should sanctify it. Now, the sanctification of life is nothing less than the dwelling of God within us; Jesus Himself thinking, feeling, acting within the soul. Holiness is the Gospel put into action. We have been meditating on the various obstacles to this supernatural life; the spirit of the world; the *ego* or self-love; and, lastly, the tempter, the evil spirit, on whose baneful influence we dwelt yesterday evening.

We have seen that all things, both within and without us, lend themselves as ready accomplices to the tempter.   In the original scheme of creation everything was intended to lead the human soul upwards unto God; from the ground on which we tread, from the flowers springing up around us, to the stars above our heads—everything spoke of God.

But since the Fall all things have become instruments in the hands of the tempter; he makes use of science to deny God ; he presents history to us as the result of purely human causes, to the exclusion, even to the defiance of Providence ; he makes use of our personality, of our imagination, for our seduction ; of our senses, to lead us astray ; he betrays us even through our heart, bidding temptation take the form of a sacrifice offered to us, or required from us.

Again, the devil makes use of religion, of piety, of certain merely conventional observances which delude even the most fervent; of petty abuses which intrude themselves into the most holy things ; he does not even scruple to make use of the altar, of the sacraments, of confession, of the Holy

Eucharist ; for, as we know, he leads the soul on to sacrilege, and makes, so to say, of God Himself an occasion of temptation.

In the midst of such dangers, what prudence should guide your steps, what vigilance direct your actions !

Hitherto, my sisters, we have but reached what may be called the threshold of the supernatural life.

Let us now advance a step farther, and consider together the elements of its very existence. If my body were separated from my soul, it would immediately fall into a state of immobility, because it would no longer have within it any principle of action; and were it necessary that it should be moved, the impulse must be communicated from some eternal agency. Life consists in an internal spring of action. The stone has no life, for, in order to give it movement, it must be taken up into the hand and thrown to a distance.

To live by faith, is to make of faith the principle of action within the soul ; and as in the soul there are many distinct impulses, such as the action of the will, the action of the heart, the action of the intellect, so faith must be the principle from which these several actions spring. In physical life, the blood circulates through all the vessels of our system, flowing from the extremities to the heart; and as the heart is in communication with the external air, the blood returns, renewed and vivified to the most distant arteries of the body.

So faith, if it be indeed the life of the soul, must circulate through the veins of the intellect and of the will; and as through the heart faith brings us into immediate communication with the Holy Spirit, so is it the vital stream constantly carrying renewed light and warmth into the inmost chamber of our being. We do not see the blood, yet it is always circulating through the human body, invisible, yet everywhere giving life. In like manner, the life of faith is not seen; it is impalpable, intangible, but it vitalizes the human soul.

Therefore, I do not like the faith which we see in some people, who attitudinize their piety, and court the attention and admiration of others. This is not the life of faith. To have the life of faith is to have within the soul the principle of faith—a principle invisible, indeed, as is our guardian angel, but which yet is ever inspiring us with good desires.

This life of faith, do we often meet with it among men? In the first place, faith itself is not always to be found. We live in an age where there is a great deal of piety, but very little faith. It is a strange fact; it may even appear a paradoxical one; but never, perhaps, were little books of devotion more numerous, never were religious practices more widely spread, never was the garb of religion more freely worn; and yet, I ask, does faith in these days penetrate deep into the souls of men, and become the essential principle of their life?

Take, for example, those who are best known to you; your husbands, brothers, relations. Is faith the mainspring of their lives? Is it not, even in those who are the strictest in complying with the external requirements of religion, a mere outside robe, suited just for Sundays and holidays? Whilst, with others, faith is but a recollection of childhood, the echo of a mother's teaching—nothing more.

And women of the world, what is their faith?

They still, indeed, believe in the catechism. They know that it is a little book transmitted from one generation to another; they hear their children stammer through it : but they never dream of reading it themselves. Faith, with them, consists in a sort of vague idea. And yet they pronounce boldly upon important religious questions ; they discuss doctrines and dogmas with wonderful fluency, and with incredible audacity and presumption scruple not to sit in judgment upon the Sovereign Pontiff, the priesthood, and upon the laws and the teaching of the Church.

Even sincere Christians, women who are frequent communicants, are not really imbued with faith. It stands, as it were, in juxtaposition, side by side, with their daily life. They know that there is an eternity, another existence ; but faith is not the vital principle, the motive power which inspires and influences them.

My sisters, it is only when faith is really living in the soul, that we can live by it. Faith must be the very essence of life; it must be to the soul, what the soul is to the body. It has been said by a holy father—and the definition is a grand one—

a Christian is a soul in a body of which the Holy Spirit forms a part. The life of faith is, not to have the Holy Spirit intermittingly, by occasional communications, by fitful gleams, but to have this same Holy Spirit, the grace of God, abiding in the heart, so that Christian belief may thus become the ruling, enlightening, and inspiring source of life.

I am not going to discuss the necessity of faith during this retreat. I take it for granted that you believe in the truths of Christianity. Nay, I am sure you do. Moreover, you know the words of our Lord, " He that believeth not shall be damned. Heaven and earth shall pass away, but My words shall not pass away."

When our Lord met with some object of compassion, or when He purposed to work a miracle, He always asked, " Dost thou believe ?"

"Dost thou believe these things?" He says to the sister of Lazarus. And, in giving His blessing to the poor woman of Canaan, He exclaims, " I have not found such great faith, no, not in Israel."

Faith, then, is the first condition of the supernatural life. To have faith is to give the adhesion of the mind, of the intellect, to revealed truth ; and this because it is the truth of God and the teaching of the Church. We must bow our intellect before the word of God and the mouth of the Church. We must believe upon the faith of the Eternal Word. The object of our faith is not the word of man, but the Eternal Word, the Word of God. Our faith is in God. What can be higher, grander? Faith is the brightest light of the world. The soul that does not believe is without light. It is faith that gives light; by it we know whence we come, and whither we go; we know the source of our life, the end of our being.

The seed buried in the bowels of the earth knows the way traced out for it through the upper crust of soil in order that it may at length germinate and blossom; the eagle knows his path through the air; the star its course through myriads of worlds in the measureless depth of space. To each is there a way appointed; and shall there be none for man? Shall man alone call upon God, and cry, "Show me my way," and God not hear?

No, my sisters, I believe in God as in a Father speaking to His child, as in One Who has drawn near to me, Whose ears have heard the beatings of my heart, Whose eyes have beheld my tears. I believe in the word of God, because I, a poor feeble child lost in the catacombs of creation, need the sound of a voicc which shall direct me, and I know that so loving a Father cannot have implanted in me one single need for which He has not also supplied au abundant satisfaction.

By the clear light of faith we are able to see how this life is but a road, a journey, a struggle; in three words, faith gives us the secret of every existence, telling us that it is for each one of us a duty to be fulfilled, a cross to be borne, an apostolate to be exercised. Life is a preparation for eternity, where life will be full, perfect, abundant, nay, even superabundant. Faith is, therefore, the grand light of life, as it is, also, the true light of society. We see nations rise up and disappear; we see a providential movement in everything. Every soul who believes, writes, as it were, afresh, that wonderful book, entitled "A Discourse upon Universal History." To the true believer, the hand of Providence is everywhere visible; to him all things are clear and light, and, standing on the mountaintops, he contemplates all that passes in the plain below. The torch of faith solves the great problems of humanity to the little child as to the aged, to the poor and ignorant as to the learned. And outside of faith, what uncertainties and questionings beset the human mind! Look at the problems which are forced upon the attention of man, and for the solution of which reason cries aloud:

" Whence is man? whither does he go?"

Human reason, bewildered and confounded, may be compared to the benighted traveller, wandering wearily along in the darkness of the night. Leaning on his staff, he gazes eagerly into the vast expanse of firmament. Nothing is to be seen but clouds, and it is a star for which he is seeking. Human reason has but the gropings of the intellect to direct it. It is without the clear light of the sun, which belongs only to faith.

Again, faith is the one great strength of life. There is no strength like that of a deep conviction. It is often said, " Happy the man who believes!" And again, " The man who has the greatest power, is the man of one idea." When the idea of the eternity of God has entered into the mind of man, when this truth has taken hold of the conscience, what strength and power does it not impart! Therefore is it that you see some heroic souls taking refuge in cloisters, in cells, throwing themselves into every field of self-devotion. Faith has, in them, attained its fullest development; their one aim is to live under its inspirations. Faith is not only the brightest light of this life, and its greatest power; it is also its sole real consolation. There is nothing sadder than a soul who does not believe.

I said yesterday that despair was the climax of all your falls, of all your sorrows. It may also be said that the climax of all human sadness is disbelief, distrust of everything. Distrust is want of faith; it is the parent of doubt, of scornful incredulity, of moral questionings. When, perhaps, some family affection disappoints or fails you, directly you lose your faith in love, you are filled with suspicion and distrust; and the human heart knows no greater sorrow than feelings such as these. If you distrust every one, even God; if you have no longer faith in God, then is your isolation complete, your sorrow absolute. You have no longer the one great consolation of life. I do not understand any consolation without faith.

Men of the world, who have experienced the trials of life, look with envy at the serenity of a Catholic sanctuary, and exclaim :

"I should be quite happy if I had faith."

It is ever and again the example I have already quoted of the man, who, in spite of all his learning, of the fame attached to his name, said, on returning to his native village, and hearing once more the prayers, the hymns, the creeds of his childhood :

"Alas for us! we reason ; but to reason is to doubt, and to doubt is to suffer."

The great consolation of life is, therefore, faith. When faith is not the mere assent of the intellect, but also its life, then all things become clear ; we comprehend not only life in general, the march of society, but we can measure the particular events of our own individual history. We know that there is a God Who numbers the hairs of our head ; we believe in the government of Providence ; we have faith in our Father, Who is in heaven ; we are at peace ; naught can befall us but what He allows ; if He permits sorrow or anxiety to fall upon us, it is because He loves us yet more than before.

The story is told of a king who, meeting a young shepherd, inquired what he earned for keeping his flock. The youth fixed his eyes upon the king, and replied:

" Sire, I earn the same as you do."

" How so? why?"

" Because, by the conduct of a flock, as by the government of men, I win heaven or hell."

Such, indeed, is the true meaning of life; the clear light of faith revealing itself to you, and showing you that all is summed up in striving to gain eternity.

When once this light has illuminated your souls, you will comprehend the beautiful words of the poor beggar, lately beatified by the Sovereign Pontiff.

One day Blessed Labre was walking along one of the roads leading to Rome; after a while he sat down by the wayside. He was clothed only in rags, and his food was but a morsel of dry bread, with muddy water, out of a wooden bowl, for his drink. Soon a joyous crowd passed by—a marriage party on their way to the wedding-feast. They stare at the poor beggar and, with a mixture of pity and disdain, exclaim:

"The unhappy wretch!"

But he rises up, and, with the dignity of the Christian who, though he may be covered but with rags, and scarce have bread enough for his daily sustenance, yet possesses within his soul the treasures of eternity, he says:

"You call me unhappy; I am very happy beneath the sunshine of the good God; none are unhappy but those who are on their road to hell."

They were grand and noble words, born of faith. When everything is judged by the standard of the supernatural, there is perfect harmony between the affections and the will; the whole human soul becomes, so to say, a hymn of praise to God.

My sisters, who are there among you who live by faith; who think that poverty is a higher good than riches; that sorrow is a greater treasure than joy; who take the gospel literally, and do not look upon it as a mere legend, a traditionary record of ideal heroism? And yet all your words and feelings ought to be inspired by faith. You must be able to say, with St. Francis of Sales:

"My God, if there be aught in me which is not inspired by faith, I will instantly root it up, and cast it out."

Your will, also, my sisters, must be brought under the control of faith's divine inspirations. The great misfortune of your life is that you do your own will, and not the will of God ; then you become a discordant note in His creation, instead of a hymn of praise to Him. If you understand the life of faith, you will show forth the praises of God.

Live, then, by faith. In this city of Lyons, where Christian traditions are still preserved, where the blood of martyrs still rises as incense to heaven, shedding the protection of its sacred perfume upon your families, let there be a living, a vigorous faith.

And now let me explain to you, my sisters, what are the duties you owe to your faith.

Your first duty is to preserve it ; and observe, never, perhaps, has faith more needed preservation than in our own days ; never have there been so many and such powerful causes at work, the tendency of which is to destroy faith. These affect every one, and you especially.

You live essentially by feeling, by sentiment; faith with you is a feeling, rather than a conviction; you hardly ever act under the austere and strong inspiration of faith; rather are you the slaves of an idea. Your natures are impulsive and uneven; a trifle elates you, a trifle casts you down. With many of you, faith is but a sensation or a remembrance; a remembrance, it may be, of your First Communion. Often it is but as a flower, of which the perfume only reaches you; or it is the fleeting impression made on you by a retreat, by some voice which for a moment held you captive; it is not the power of earnest conviction penetrating into the very depths of the soul.

But side by side with this danger from within, which you may avoid, there is also danger from without.

How foreign, how antagonistic, even to faith, are the ideas and opinions of the present day! Men will have nothing now but the exterior of Christianity. They like Christian civilization—the varnish of Christianity, so to say—but they do not rest upon its fundamental basis.

Look at what is now going on in the world. What is the reading of the day? It frightens me to see the bad books, the godless papers, the dangerous publications, which cover the tables, and fill the book-shelves of Christian women. Everything against the Church is greedily welcomed. The consequence is, a deterioration of the intellect to an extent that causes abuse of the Church to be but too easily believed, and her bitterest enemies courted and praised. With a marvellous facility, these books and pamphlets diffuse themselves, carrying with them a certain familiarity with divine things, which penetrates into every grade of society, appealing to every intelligence, and fastening itself upon every soul! We must confess that the virgin purity, the strict orthodoxy of faith exists no more. The exquisite delicacy of truth is no longer understood.

One thing, in these latter days, has deeply humiliated us, Christian bishops and priests, who love the Church with all her conflicts, all her greatness, all her virtues and good works; it has humiliated us to see to what an extent a simple word which fell from the lips of the Sovereign Pontiff has been misunderstood. The Head of of the Church did but say this:

" That Jesus Christ must be the corner-stone of society, that Jesus Christ has rights, that the rights of God are somewhat higher than the rights of man." Nothing more than this; the common teaching of the catechism.

And behold! the world calls it a modern discovery, a strange invention; the cry is taken up and sung in every key. And we see not only doctors of science, but even Christian women, who, perhaps, have been in the morning with veiled faces to receive Jesus Christ in Holy Communion, going forth in the evening, and citing before the bar of their childish intelligence and feeble reason, the words of the Father of the faithful, to question and too often to contradict them.

Is there not danger to faith in such things?

Therefore, my sisters, it is that you must preserve your faith by abstaining from dangerous and harmful reading.

A woman, very reprehensible, on account of the

books which she has published, and who, by the seductive brilliancy of her style, has worked grievous mischief both in the hearts and the intellects of her readers—this woman writes in one of her novels: " Faith enters into the soul that suffers, and doubt draws nigh to the soul that dreams."

These words are most true. Suffering, it may be said, is often the road to faith ; but doubt takes possession of the soul of the dreamer.

Women, nowadays especially, love day-dreams, unhealthy reading, fantastic imaginations, exaggerated conceptions, everything, in fact, which produces excitement ; and, instead of confining themselves to solid, substantial reading, they feed on books which endanger their faith, and lead them on to ruin.

My sisters, remember these words :

" Faith descends into the soul which suffers ; doubt draws nigh to the soul which dreams."

Let then the choice of your reading be such as will conduce to the preservation of your faith, and I add also, be careful for the preservation of your faith in conversation. It is impossible to escape the influence of the words we hear, and grave is the responsibility of those who utter them.

Few minds are rich enough to live upon their own resources ; upon the ideas they have acquired, the greater number feed only upon what they hear. If an objection, an accusation against the faith be laid down, they are at once subjugated or fascinated by it. You give little heed to this : but everywhere around you, anti-Christian ideas are rife ; the husband to whom your life is linked, your sons, your brothers, perhaps even your sisters are more or less impregnated with these heterodox views upon religion and the Church. You live in this atmosphere, you have to carry the fragile plant of faith in a vase more fragile still, and without continual watchfulness, this faith will fade and die. Pray then with the apostles—" Lord, increase my faith."

St. Francis of Sales, who had been compelled to spend his life in the midst of the conflicts of heresy, used to say :

" My God, I thank Thee that I have been able to pass with a firm step, and without failing, through all these *deleterious* doctrines."

And when asked on his death-bed whether he

had ever had any doubts, he replied: " Doubts! no; I have always believed with the simplicity of a child; it was my delight to believe; I die in the same catholic faith which I have loved, which I have preached, for which I would give my life."

Such is the one cry of strong and vigorous souls; amidst the dangers of their existence they have preserved their faith. But there is a second duty before you; you must nourish your faith. I have already said that in these days there is piety, but not much faith. Together with many admirable works of Christian literature there appear every day little pious books full of notes of admiration and of interrogation, of vapid phrases and high-flown exaggerated expressions, books I mean such as you open and sometimes use in your thanksgivings after Communion.

Too many souls are fed on such—I will not call them mental products, they do not deserve the name—but on such wretched trash only tolerated because it is on a par with the intellect of the age. Devout souls are thus reduced to a poverty of intellectual food, the shallowness of which can hardly be concealed by the sonorous words and pompous phrases and expressions with which these publications abound.

Such is the present state of things, my sisters. There is much activity and excitement about in the world; you will find in some a sort of angular piety perhaps, but solid, earnest, intelligent faith is the one thing wanting.

Formerly, faith was a family tradition. Mothers read the good solid books which teach the science of Christianity; men belonging to secular professions, magistrates, *savants*, even, studied the Holy Scriptures and theology along with the works treating of their own particular branch of learning. In our days, theological studies have been abandoned, nothing remains but a profound ignorance of the things of God in the soul of man.

I want to convince you, my sisters, of the necessity of preserving your faith, and of giving it a real comprehension of holy things. Religion is the essence of all that is true and beautiful and good. Read good books; read the works of the saints; drink in the manly vigorous force of their thoughts. Never indulge in dangerous reading. Say in the words of Holy Scripture: "Give me understanding, Lord, and I shall live."

May God grant you the gift of faith.

Do you really understand the Christian doctrines, the holy teachings of the Liturgy? Oh! did you but comprehend the grand lessons of faith! They contain treasures of which you are utterly ignorant. I was reading over, for instance, the other day, for my own private edification, the ritual of the administration of the sacrament of holy orders; I know of no prayers more full of poetical inspiration, of life-giving beauty. Why do Christians allow such things as these to lie by unknown? Why do they not seek therein the light and the fire which would give strength to their own souls?

Feed your minds, then, with solid reading; attend the sermons in your parish churches; go sometimes even to the catechisings. These things are not intended only for children and servants. You may be in greater need of them perhaps than they; many a poor girl who has attended regularly a course of instruction would be perfectly capable of teaching you many things of which you are ignorant.

Catholic truth is so full of marvels, it may be studied ever and again without being exhausted; it is like the well of Jacob, of which the waters spring up into everlasting life. Listen with simplicity to the Word of God; and thus you will nourish your faith.

Your third duty is to propagate your faith. I do not mean that you must set yourselves up as preachers, or arguers; but you may both defend and propagate the faith by your activity, by your good works, by your self-devotion, and especially by the earnestness of your own convictions.

A believing soul is like the sun behind a cloud; in spite of the darkness which hides and overshadows it, its rays yet shine through the clouds and give them brightness and light. Thus does the inward presence of earnest faith within the soul seem to clothe even the outward form with something of its own light and beauty.

There is nothing more sweet, more exquisite, than a soul thus revealing itself through the manifestation of faith, for faith is the charm, the perfume of life. And therefore the power which carries conviction is not always that of words, and of demonstration; it is that of a living, of an incarnate faith; that of a Christian woman wearing Christianity nobly, understanding how to live upon the great and grand traditions of Jesus Christ, and then to impart them to others.

During the terrible wars which have of late devastated the United States, events took place which are but little known, and which yet have in them much which may serve for our edification. A considerable number of Protestant soldiers, wounded on the field of the battle, and carried into the hospitals, there became Catholics.

The Bishop of Charlestown told me that out of twenty Protestant soldiers brought into the hospitals eighteen died Catholics, converted by conversations they had held with the sisters of St. Charles and of St. Joseph who had nursed them; and the same prelate related to me a very encouraging and touching fact.

An old officer was brought into the hospital in a dying state; he had never thought of religion. The sister said to him:

"You are going to die, turn your thoughts to God."

He replied : " I have never thought of Him for forty years, what do you think He can do with me ? I know Him but little, and He perhaps knows me still less."

The sister was not discouraged, she added, " You must learn to know God ; He is a Father."

And she continued to speak to him in the persuasive words of deep conviction, and then asked him, " Are you a Catholic or a Protestant ?"

" I do not exactly know," replied the officer, " but I dare say I am a Protestant."

" Shall I send for a Catholic priest ?" asked the sister.

The officer answered, " Which is your religion, sister ?"

" The Catholic religion."

" Then bring me your priest."

The sister sent for a priest from Charlestown. He came to the bed of the dying man and asked him, " Do you believe that there is a God ?"

" Yes, I believe that there is a God, Who created the world."

" Do you believe in three Persons in one God ?"

" I do not know."

The priest explained, and the dying man turning to the sister, said, "Do you believe this?"

"Yes," she said.

"I do also," said the officer.

The priest then spoke of the mysteries of the Incarnation and Redemption. At each explanation the sick man looked at the sister of charity, asking: "Do you believe this?" And on her answering in the affirmative he too said, "I believe!"

All the great Christian doctrines were thus gone through, and the dying man made a complete profession of faith on the authority of the sister of charity whose noble self-devotion he had understood and admired. There is something incomparably beautiful in this story; charity gives birth to faith; faith lives by charity according to the beautiful words of St. Paul; the Gospel incarnate in the soul of man upon the affirmation of the Church.

Well! my sisters, in the terrible medley of conflicting opinions, in the deadly struggle between mind and mind of which our unhappy Europe is the scene, there are even more souls crushed and wounded, stricken unto death than there were soldiers lying dying and dead on the bloody field of America. Oh! were there but souls full of faith, earnest, loving, living souls, the world would soon be conquered and transformed ; for there is no power in the world greater than that of a soul full of light from above, devoting herself for the faith with all the tenderness and the self-immolation which inspired the sacrifice of Jesus Christ. There is nothing more powerful than truth made visible through a life of charity.

Go forth then, into the world to the conquest of souls. After having preserved your own faith, after having strengthened and vivified it, and made it the loadstone of your life, bear away the light to the souls who have it not, and believe that to give faith is to give more than material bread to the poor, for it is to give the bread of the soul, it is to give joy and comfort to the heart, it is to give the very treasure of life, it is, in fact, to give all that is highest and greatest in the world, "hope and love."

Life of Sacrifice.

"Ought not Christ to suffer?"—St. Luke xxiv. 26.

THIS morning, my sisters, I endeavoured to direct your thoughts to one of the constituent elements of the supernatural life—I spoke of the life of faith.

The second element of the supernatural life, following upon faith, is sacrifice; and this evening, my sisters, I would speak to you of the life of sacrifice.

The word is, indeed, a fearful one to human nature. It provokes reason to indignation, the senses to rebellion. Sacrifice! Yet is it the great law of heaven and of earth; and, since the fall, the one supreme law. Before the fall even sacrifice existed; not bloody, not painful, but existing, *even as labour existed*, for man, in the midst of the joys of the earthly paradise, was not condemned to sterile immobility. Neither shall we, when we come to the ecstasy of heaven, be sunk in barren and unfruitful idleness. The soul is essentially active, even as God, Who is absolute activity, pure action.

Work and sacrifice existed before the fall. To offer sacrifice to God, is to recognize His sovereignty, to acknowledge Him as Master.

It would seem an easy thing, my sisters, to acknowledge that God is the Master, to accept His rights, to confess His pre-eminence. To say that God is our Master, who is there who does not do it? Who dares to dispute His sovereignty, His supreme authority over us? Who dreams of questioning this? No one apparently, every one really. When you withhold the thoughts of your heart from Him; nay, more, when you go farther, and allow your heart to stray away after dangerous and forbidden affections, you are refusing to God His sovereignty over you. Sin is nothing else than the soul setting itself above God, destroying His original scheme, rejecting the harmony which He has established, not accepting the sovereignty of

His laws. Every sinful act denies, contests, and sometimes attempts to overthrow, the sovereignty of God.

Yet God demands the acknowledgment of His sovereignty. You yourselves, my sisters, in your own homes, unless you are deplorably weak, unless you go down upon your knees before your children, and are governed by little majesties of fifteen; even you do not allow your authority to be contested and discussed, you know how to make it respected when it is infringed upon by those who ought to obey. You are right in not allowing your sceptre to fall into these childish hands. And God, God the Father of the human family, God the Creator of the universe, can you admit that His sovereignty should not be acknowledged? The sovereignty of God is acknowledged only through sacrifice. It may, indeed, be said that since the fall, death alone has borne witness to this sovereignty. When man has been able to offer his life, and laying it down at the feet of God, has said, "This life, I immolate it. I would pour it out. It is but a drop of water on the sands of immensity. Thou art, O God, the Lord of the world, the Lord

of my being, Thou hast right over me!"   The
means of confessing the sovereignty of God, is
death ; sacrifice, which is but the passage from life
to death.

In the old world, the heathen themselves instinctively, in virtue of that tradition imbedded in the
heart of man, brought victims to the altar, and put
them to death, to the glory of God. What was
there in this act of destruction, in the blood thus
shed within the temple ?   There was a hymn of
praise confessing the sovereignty of God. Sacrifice
is the acknowledgment that God is Lord.   Do you
want a proof of this ? Whenever sacrifice ceases
to be, when it is put away, the rights of God are,
little by little, forgotten and denied. In our days,
Christians are alarmed at the audacious, the de-
structive, let me even say, the fatal, negations with
which men assail our Lord and God ! Why are
the rights of God thus disregarded, why is God
Himself, as it were, put aside as some far-fetched
ideal, only fit for the cradle of ancient generations ?
It is because, in non-Catholic doctrines, there is
neither sacrifice nor altar. When sacrifice exists
no longer, when the altar is destroyed, and the

divine Master banished, God, His rights, and His sovereignty are no longer acknowledged.

ˎ There is a fatal progression in error; the rights of God are denied when sacrifice ceases to exist. There is but one indestructible society, holding a divine, a blessed mission, preserving, proclaiming, defending, affirming the rights of God ; it is the great Catholic commonwealth, going on its way through time and space, bearing everywhere the sacrificial victim, and chanting ever the glory of God.

The attestation of the rights of God is sacrifice. When the time came that these rights were to be affirmed and made manifest to the eye of humanity, then did the Son of God come down from heaven upon the earth. He said to His Father, "A victim is necessary! here I am." And he gave Himself up to die on the Cross.

And henceforth sacrifice in man is seen in its true greatness, and all human actions in their real significance. Let a man, be he ever so poor, ever so miserable, if he is ascending the road to Calvary, bringing with him, it may be, but a straw ; yet if this straw be laid upon the blood-stained Cross of the

Redeemer, that man will obtain power and glory which will win for him an everlasting crown. If we cast into this crucible, this sacrificial fire, but one tear, one sigh, one prayer, one secret immolation, some one innermost self-annihilation—all these shall have their echoes in eternity, and await us in everlasting glory.

Sacrifice is the great law, the fundamental law of Christianity, and every soul desirous of regeneration, every soul that wills to live the life of Christ, or to have in itself the supernatural life, must build its existence upon sacrifice.

In our days, do people think of building upon sacrifice? of giving this tendency to education? No; they are only pre-occupied with the wish of putting away all sorrow and all care. And that is why many young girls enter upon marriage, and after two or three years of domestic life exclaim, " Oh, if I had but known that marriage had so many great sorrows and sacrifices, I would never have joined my hands and bowed my head to receive the nuptial benediction." This is because you, mothers, have educated them with the idea of the pleasure, the triumph of ruling a house, but not with the idea of sacrifice. This is how you mould, so to speak, your children in their early years. You give way to their caprices; you leave their natures uncontrolled. You do not understand that you ought to form, to discipline them to sacrifice; that if you do not, the day will come when they must be disciplined through a sorrow sharp and terrible, which they will hardly be able to, endure, because they have not been prepared beforehand for the great trials of life.

The law of sacrifice is the fundamental law of Christianity, the true law of life. The soul that would live must fulfil this law in its own being.

Our Lord said to His disciples, when He entrusted them with His divine mission, " Unless the grain of wheat falling into the ground die, itself remaineth alone. But if it die, it bringeth forth much fruit."

To learn to die to oneself, this is the power which can fertilize and regenerate. To die to oneself, to annihilate self—this is the great law of Christianity. Who consents to offer sacrifice ? We are afraid of it. We are afraid of dying to ourselves. We are afraid of self-immolation. We will not sacrifice ourselves !

The priest to whom you have revealed the state of your soul, asks of you, perhaps, some small sacrifice. He asks it in that spirit of fatherly tenderness which God has put into his heart, and often he has even to dispute with you whether your soul shall belong to Satan or to God. You say, "We are incapable of such sacrifices." You will not renounce the frivolities, the trifles which make up your life; you think you have done a great deal if you have diminished the width of your skirts by an inch, if you have cut off a little of the splendour of your dress, if you have done God the honour to bow down before Him for a few minutes, and uttered a careless sigh in His presence.

These are the sacrifices which some make, and call themselves Christians; they fancy they have understood the meaning of life, and have penetrated into the very depths of Christianity! It is enough to make one smile with pity, if not weep with compassion, to behold souls thus needing to be led back to the great law of Calvary, to the one only fruitful, the one only true law, the law of sacrifice.

But there are treasures of mercy in God. He

knows that you will not, of yourselves, consent to sacrifice, to self-immolation, that every step of the ground in your heart has to be disputed, ere He win to Himself the surrender of your prayers, of your reading, of your luxury, of your actions, even of your family devotion. Then how does God work? He says, "This soul is sick, it must go to the hospital."

What is that hospital whither God sends the souls that are sick? It is that of suffering. He takes you there, He makes you lie down upon that bed of blessing, the bed of suffering. Until now, you looked upon suffering as a curse; you murmured at it when it visited you; you understood not that God then vouchsafed to descend from His eternity, and, like the good Samaritan, to take you in His arms, to tend and heal you; for it is through the mighty power of suffering that God brings sanctification, and life, and salvation to the soul.

Let me show you, my sisters, the mysterious relations, the coincidence between sacrifice and suffering. It is most certain that sufferings exist around us; that they fall upon us, swifter, thicker than flakes of snow on a winter's day. Suffering bears a message from God to him who endures it ; suffering is the great power of God, the medicine wherewith He heals the soul.

What is it that we need in life ? I have said it already ; we need light and strength, in other words, we need sanctification. When God sends suffering, He sends that which is, after faith, the great light of life, and often suffering is the highway to faith. I quoted this morning a very worldly author, a woman who yet found in the inspiration of her own thought these words, " The soul that suffers is nigh to faith ; the soul that dreams is nigh to doubt." Yes, suffering may become the great highway that leads to faith.

Look at that man of the world. Everything has succeeded with him ; he has been nurtured in health and wealth ; his affairs have prospered ; God has given him a wife who is the delight of his life ; his children are growing up around him in health and happiness ; he has all the joys, all the honours of life ; he is honest and upright ; his integrity wins him public esteem ; there is room in his heart for all, his children, his family, those who are in any way brought into relation with him ; he is ever forward in good works. He has a thought for everybody, everything, excepting God ; He is the great forgotten one. To Him he never looks in the morning ; to Him he never turns at night ; he ignores God ; he never thinks of Him.

And yet, what is there which has not spoken to him of God ? In childhood, when he came into the world, he saw the sun declaring the glory of God ; he played upon that green carpet of the earth, where grew the flowers which his infant hands delighted to pluck ; his mother watched over his early years, she taught him to kneel down and to pray to his Father in heaven. Later on he came to the priest, he heard the voice of the Church, he learned the doctrine of Christ. Yet God is still the One Being forgotten. And if you go through the cities of this old Europe of ours, how many men will you not find for whom God is the one Thing forgotten, forsaken ! Neither the thunder of heaven, nor the events of earth, nor the anxious cares of the clergy avail to bring them back to God.

But a day comes when God overthrows the

fortunes of this prosperous man; death carries off one of his children, clouds gather upon his brow; he becomes sad, depressed, desolate; he murmurs at times, until at length memory awakens, and the instinctive cry of suffering nature bursts from him, "My God! my God!" Suffering is indeed for many the only light which leads to life.

Or else, it may be, that we see a frivolous soul, one who does not, indeed, forget God, but who does not love Him; who gives Him but a vague and passing thought, and no real love or tenderness of heart. Well, all has been in vain to recall this soul to God: the loving entreaties of children or friends, the warnings of the preacher, the threatenings of eternity, all are in vain. God smites her, and she too cries out, "My God! my God!" True light has come to her, showing her the fragility of all earthly things, and revealing to her, beyond present anguish, the brightening dawn of eternity. Sorrow is the great light of life, shining upon the souls, which, through it, are being made ready for willing sacrifice.

And by suffering God gives also strength to the soul. Of what is that soul capable which has never suffered ? What does it know of the providential laws of Christianity ? What of life ? only its joys. What of its own strength ? it has never battled, never been tried. What does it know of self, of life, of God ? The soul which has never suffered knows nothing, it has no strength, it has passed through no struggles, no trials.

I am obliged to hurry on, only giving you the heads of thoughts.

Suffering is also the expiation of sin. We too easily forget that God demands expiation. Jesus Christ has bequeathed to us His sufferings, that we may be made capable of expiation. You have offended God ; do you think there is nothing required of you ? Do you think that the rapid absolution which just soothes your conscience is enough to bestow sanctifying grace upon your souls ? Do you think that the consequences of evil, the effects of sin, need no expiation ? And so, because we are cowardly, because we are without strength, without energy for self-revenge, God takes upon Himself the care of the expiation we owe to Him.

Therefore He lays upon us the providential penance of suffering. Oh, did you but know how to accept suffering, how grand is such an expiation!

If the woman who feels that her life is broken, whose heart is sinking under the daily consciousness of being misunderstood, whose soul is sorely tried, whose conscience, perhaps, is burdened : if, instead of parading her griefs, of decking herself as a victim, she were to offer her sufferings to God, to mingle her tears with those of Jesus, how great would be her power of expiation, not only for herself, but for those around her !

And supposing, even, that you are innocent yourselves, it may be that those you love have offended God, and if they do not return to the paths of virtue, it is, perhaps, because you have not as yet suffered enough.

All suffering is an altar, upon which we may become, as it were, a victim for the souls of others. How many hearts have had the courage of self-immolation that they might atone for the faults of those they loved.

To suffer is to expiate ; to suffer is to merit ; to suffer is yet more, to love.

Yes, to suffer is to love. When Jesus Christ

was born in a stable, in the manger, when He suffered, when He gave Himself to the cross: it was out of love for His Father; He was thus uttering the cry of divine tenderness, "I love Thee, O Father!" And when our Lord said, "My God, why hast Thou forsaken Me?" it was, as it were, the cry of despairing tenderness. In suffering there is love.

Is there any love in our careless prayers? Have you ever made one earnest act of love to God, save when you have performed some deed of sacrifice, or come to the holy Table, and taken the sacred Substance into your hearts? Oh, yes! then, indeed, did you fulfil one great act of love.

None may escape the law of sacrifice, any more than the law of death. Death is the great sacrifice; suffering is as inevitable as death. The truth is, we do not believe in death; death is for all, excepting for us; we delude ourselves; in vain does one funeral procession after another pass before our eyes; we persist in fancying that death is going farther away from us. As the child climbs the mountain, believing that he will at last reach the blue sky, so you, as you advance in life, believe that death is farther from you. It is said that the earth moves through space with a rapidity that is appalling; well, then, death is approaching us with no less rapidity—with a rapidity exceeding, if I may so express myself, that of a railway train rushing onwards with headlong speed.

You are one of a crowd which is hurrying on to death, to eternity; you cannot escape this great law, any more than you can that of suffering. Suffering is the beginning of death, as death is the completion of sacrifice. As in the Mass there is the preparation and the completion of the sacrifice, so in suffering there is both the preparation and the consummation.

If you do not suffer for Jesus Christ, you will suffer in opposition to Jesus Christ. The history of Calvary will be the blessing of him who suffers for Jesus; it will be the curse of him who suffers in opposition to Christ.

There are three places whither God sends suffering; three tabernacles of sorrow, if I may so say. There is the tabernacle where suffering has no merit, because then human liberty has ceased to exist, grace is exhausted, and the fate of the soul has been fixed for all eternity; it is hell, the first tabernacle of suffering, which still forms part of the divine plan, glorifying the justice of God, in those who have refused to glorify His goodness. There is the tabernacle of purgatory, where the souls who will be hereafter summoned to glory perfect their expiation, and acquire that purity which shall fit them for heaven. Lastly, there is the tabernacle of earth, where the value of suffering is well-nigh infinite, because it moves the heart of Jesus Christ.

Thus great is the power of suffering, even in this life. You obtain more by one tear than by orders and authority. Your tears are the symbols of your power, for you employ them to secure your dominion. The tears shed by humanity, and ascending to God, have in them the mighty power which wins heaven. To know how to suffer is the great secret of life; it is to understand the law of Christianity, the law of sacrifice.

I repeat it: you cannot escape this law, and if you do not suffer for Jesus, you suffer against Him.

Does not the world, my sisters, exact sacrifices from you ?   The sacrifice, it may be, of your health, of your fortune, the sacrifice of your time, the sacrifice even of your happiness ; you are for ever wearing yourselves out in seeking to please the world ; I have often thought that an essay might be written, a satirical one indeed, but a most amusing one (if you will forgive the word), drawing a comparison between the Lent of the world and the Lent of God ; and it would then be seen on which side there were, in reality, the greatest sacrifices.

Ah ! I know how easily you cast aside the sacrifices of the Church's Lent. But this just proves that you refuse to accept the law of sacrifice, the law of suffering. And yet the more you give yourselves up unreservedly to the world, the more will you have of secret sufferings ; the more will your feelings be wounded, your sensitiveness aggrieved ; the more will you be tormented by the stings of jealousy, and tortured by anxiety and remorse. None may escape the law of suffering and of sacrifice.

Learn then to accept the law of sacrifice ; to let yourselves be disciplined by God ; this law is God's discipline, the discipline of suffering. What is the burden laid upon us, priests? We try by the sword of the Spirit and the hammer of Christian doctrine, to drive the truth into souls called by God to the participation of heavenly joys; but we are power‑less, for you oppose yourselves to our success, and make our efforts vain.

And yet the soul only becomes great through suffering. The higher, the more sensitive the soul, the greater is she, and the greater is her capacity for suffering. Women are formed to suffer more keenly than men, from the greater susceptibility of their nature. Learn then, my sisters, to suffer in a spirit of holiness.

Two instances recur to my mind : one relates to St. Frances of Romagna. She was rich, and won-drously beautiful; when still young she became a widow and lost all her wealth. Thus smitten by grief she could yet say with exquisite tenderness to God: "Lord, Thou gavest me all; Thou hast taken all from me; Thy name be praised." This was her chief prayer.

The other relates to that noble woman, whom the Church has for a century venerated as a saint, and whose gentle memory is recalled by this day's solemnity—Madame de Chantal. Her youth, too, had been brilliant, her fortune considerable; a widow at thirty, she retired, with the children she had to bring up, to the castle of one of her relations. There mortification in its most trying aspect meets her; she finds herself insulted in the home, at the table, which should have been her own, ill-treated by the inferiors of the household. Ten years did she remain in this position, never complaining, ever gentle and kind. Last year I made a pilgrimage to that home, still redolent with the perfume of her sainted memory. A little path was pointed out to me, along which she was wont to pass, carrying help to the sick and desolate in their wretched homes. The people about said to me: "You are come to visit the memorials of *our good lady.*" For nigh upon three centuries this name has survived through all changes, all vicissitudes; she is still called "*the good lady.*" I went and knelt down in the little church where she had worshipped God. There is still there an altar-cloth which is the work of her hands, and I was told "*the good lady*" did this. God beheld her working here with other ladies who were also the glory of the Church.

Nothing is great save through sacrifice and suffering. The whole of Christianity is contained in sacrifice. In the liturgy there is a word which is identical with sacrifice, it is the word *action*. Do you think that the priest exists only for preaching? Too often you make us into mere preachers, into stage orators. We do not exist only to preach, but to go up to the altar to offer sacrifice, to bow down, to do that which in Catholic language is so well called the *action*, to take the victim, to confess the sovereignty of God, and to offer Jesus to Him, for the salvation of souls.

Every Christian woman may be a priest in her own family; she has an altar to which she may ascend. This altar is her heart; and there, as she presents her offerings of self-sacrifice, of self-devotion, will she obtain blessings without number, without compare.

When the Church is in peril, when in the midst of the desolations of the age we behold the tide of unbelief rising, we stay ourselves upon the tabernacle, we take Jesus Christ, and we find strength.

Were there in the world but one priest with the bread for consecration and the wine for transubstantiation, this priest would still hold the greatest power on earth; fortune, power, the authority to command, nothing equals the power of the priest, even although alone, lost, isolated in the depths of catacombs, or in the desert, when in his hands he bears Jesus Christ. All else is earth; Jesus is heaven.

My sisters, you mistake your true power. You believe it to be pleasure; you think it lies in your dress, in your features, in your wit, your drawing-rooms, your books; you believe, in short, that power is enjoyment; remember that enjoyment leads to death, and sacrifice alone to life which shall be everlasting.

Life of Union with God.

"I will pour out upon the house of David the spirit of grace and supplication."—Zach. xii. 10.

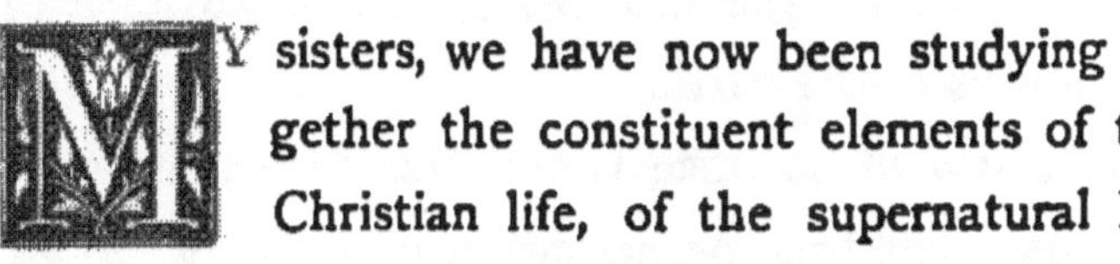

Y sisters, we have now been studying together the constituent elements of the Christian life, of the supernatural life in the soul. I have shown you how to overcome the obstacles to this life, the world, self, and the evil spirit; and I have proved to you that the first element of this supernatural life is a spirit of faith, of a living, firm, holy, austere, and ardent faith. People are apt to content themselves with piety, and to stop short of faith. Faith must be living, it must be active within us; it must be the guiding compass of the frail bark of your life; the light which enlightens, the power which protects it. You must guard your faith from any books or conversations which might undermine it ; and you must propagate your faith by imparting to the souls of unbelievers the happiness of your own convictions.

I added that the second element in this life was the spirit of sacrifice. Christianity is built upon sacrifice ; the world, since its regeneration, rests only on sacrifice ; in all things, progress is developed only by sacrifice. The germination which gives fecundity to the grain of corn, as Jesus Christ tells us, springs from the fact that it dies unto itself in the bowels of the earth.

This law of sacrifice is but the perpetuation of Calvary ; but this perpetuation of Calvary would be insufficient unless it were referred to Jesus ; unless you yourselves are in direct communication with Him. Were Jesus alone, you would have no participation either in His beauty or in His glory, Jesus desires to put Himself in communication with you by the sacraments in which He meets you, by the sacrifices which He imposes upon you ; He desires that every soul should be, in some sort, a Calvary. Every soul is a tabernacle. When you go to Communion, our Lord leaves the silence in which He is enshrouded, and passes into your souls; then are you in direct, intimate, living communication with Him. Yet is this not enough, you must have a Calvary within yourselves; Calvary must be perpetuated, applied, individualized within you. You cannot escape the law of sacrifice, which is fulfilled by suffering.

I said yesterday that were a comparision to be drawn between the sacrifices imposed upon you by the world, and those demanded from you by Jesus Christ, it would be seen that the world's sacrifices are incomparably more numerous, incomparably heavier, harder, and more trying than those asked of you by Jesus.

Well, indeed, might the spirit of the world be expressed by the words: "My yoke is hard, and my burthen heavy."

The yoke of the world is hard, for it demands the sacrifice of your intellect, which it nourishes only on frivolity; of your heart, which it delivers over to passion, holding up to scorn every innocent, pure and holy feeling; the world will even take from you your reputation, and your home affections; heavy, indeed, is the yoke, intolerable the burden laid upon you by the world.

Jesus asks of you only the sacrifice of that which is unlawful within you, of that which lowers, degrades, tortures you ; and in asking this, Jesus is working for you and for your happiness, whereas the world is always against your real interests. This is what I showed yesterday.

Oh ! did you but thoroughly understand the life of faith and the life of sacrifice, you would be true and earnest Christians. The soul that has within it the light of faith, the spirit of sacrifice, is both great and generous.

This morning I desire, if possible, to go yet deeper into the practice of the Christian life ; to make you realize, if possible, what is the life of union with God.

This is the third step in the supernatural life.

Did I but preach to you faith, it were insufficient, just as sacrifice would often be too crushing for your weak nature; the two, must, as it were, be linked together and crowned by one great supreme consolation—union with God.

Let me, then, tell you what is this life of union with God. It is the first step in your eternal life, in eternal union, in eternal joy. Would you not make of this world the beginning of heaven? Would you not be creatures prepared for eternity, seeds of paradise? For we are destined to be the seeds either of everlasting joy, or of everlasting misery. If within us there be but the sap of this world, we become the dry, accursed wood, which bears no fruit, but will be cut down for everlasting fire; but if we imbibe the sap of grace, we shall grow, and flourish unto everlasting happiness.

You must, then, have this union with God, which is heaven begun on earth. I purpose to show what this life of union really is, adding that it needs but to have a little more love in our hearts to move us to give ourselves to God, and to our Lord Jesus Christ. There are three terms in the life of union with God; the vision of God, intercourse with God, and at the same time the adherence, so to say, of our nature to Him, or union with God.

My sisters, I already hear the objections which many amongst you will immediately raise. "What! see God! But God is the Invisible, how shall we attain to Him? how take hold of Him? We may try to follow Him in our dreams beyond the clouds; but it is a vain pursuit in the fields of the ideal, in the realms of fancy. How can we see God?

The Gospel gives a sublime answer, which in itself is a whole revelation: " Blessed are the pure in heart, for they shall see God."

Purity is the eye which reveals God to us. The world does not see God, because the world is not pure; the angels are pure, and they see God. The want of purity causes a cloud to rise between the eyes of the soul and God, between the Sun Eternal and the light of the intellect: when a cloud passes over the sun it is no longer seen.

Can we on this our earth see God? Yes; not, indeed, as in heaven, as we shall see Him beyond the grave; but we see God darkly, as in a glass, says St. Paul. As the fiery glow of the sun is seen in the water, so may we, even through His creation, apprehend God.

Purity is the eye which beholds God. The purer the soul, the more will she see God; the more we are able to detach ourselves from self, from the flesh, from the affections which draw the heart down to earth, the more we can ascend the divine heights of purity, the more shall we be able to see God, and to realize the beautiful words of Holy Scripture: "Blessed are the pure in heart, for they shall see God."

Purity is the dominion of the soul over all that is earthly; the government of the spiritual over the material; the supremacy of the intellect over matter. As the soul ascends more and more to the heights of purity, she draws nearer to God; from purity she derives a strength which is superior to all other—the very intellect of the pure in heart gains fresh expansion. Would that you, like the Church, could study the marvels which take place in the world of souls. How often does the priest fall on his knees in humble thankfulness for the demonstration of Christian truth which has been given him!

You are often troubled by doubts; questionings torment you; faith flits before your eyes, it has not the clearness which you need, you crave for more certainty, more demonstration. As for me, since God has blessed me by bringing me into intimate contact with the souls of others, I have vividly apprehended the truth of eternal realities.

There is not a word in the Gospel which has not its own living demonstration incarnate within the soul. "Blessed are the pure in heart, for they shall see God."

I am not speaking of the great minds which have been illustrious in catholic theology, and who, as they have grown in purity, have penetrated deeper into the essence of God; but I might mention the Angel of the schools, who possessing so pre-eminently both faith and divine learning, raised in their honour that noble monument which has been the admiration of ages. St. Peter's at Rome, the Cathedral of Cologne, are spoken of as monuments of incomparable grandeur. They are, in truth, immense creations, admirable both as wholes and in their details; they have been erected to the glory of God, to the honour of the Christian faith. Yet grand as these monuments are, they are as nothing by the side of the "Summa Theologia" of St. Thomas Aquinas. This great man had renounced his wealth, he had concealed his name beneath the cloak of poverty; he had overcome the temptations which assailed his youth, and God permitted heaven to open out to him, and angels came down and girded his loins with the girdle of purity. So then it is purity which built up the greatest, noblest monument of human intellect, that monument of divine science to which none other, as a philosopher has said, may be compared. It is the monument of faith, erected by purity.

There are other pure hearts which have no literary life, no learning, no relations with the world of intellect, who yet leave behind them a witness to the power of purity. Marie Eustelle, a poor, humble seamstress, appeared some years since in the diocese of La Rochelle; she could barely read or write; but, having grown up in the spirit of purity and faith, she has left behind her pages which shine, not, indeed, with the marvels and the splendour of literary science, but with the clear light of purity of heart. She apprehended, she understood God; her purity was to her as the eye of the soul, wherewith she was able to see Him. A great cardinal, in undertaking the publication of the volumes containing the inspirations of this holy maiden, declared that her works were most edifying and theological, showing that, all unlettered as she was, she had yet, through the splendour of her virginal purity, beheld the essence of God.

But, unfortunately, we too commonly find this divine power of purity rejected. You have examples of this everywhere around you ; it is as a judgment of God falling upon the human race. When is it that your sons make shipwreck of their faith ? that they, as it were, receive the baptism of infidelity ? Not so long as they are pure. It may be said that in man faith and purity walk ever side by side. They are two sisters, two angels, going hand in hand, with wings entwined—they are inseparable ; for if the one be driven away, the other soon takes flight. They rarely subsist apart ; if they do, it is with more or less of diminished power. It is one of the laws of the human heart, one of the laws of human nature, that things supernatural and divine are seen only by purity.

Doubtless our age has its own splendour and greatness, its virtues and its wonderful works. As a great bishop, in drawing a comparison between the past and present age, once said : " The growth of Christian enterprise in this century is wonderful." Everywhere in the world some manifestation of the

Church is seen. Yet by the side of that which is good in society, we see the working of evil. Two great sounds alone are now heard in the world; the sound of your concerts, of your assemblies, of your amusements, and the sound of your machinery. Machinery, and the sweat of toil, in order to provide a little bread for the hardworked poor woman; fêtes, pleasures, concerts, wherewith to charm the idleness of the rich, cultivated woman, who asks only to enjoy life! What is to be done? Our present century is full of clouds. God is no longer known. And so sophists and writers of bad books spring up and spread abroad those audacious anonymous pages which assail the existence of God, and of Jesus Christ.

When purity no longer exists, God is denied and insulted. There is a necessary relation between purity of soul and the vision of God.

Unless the heart be pure, it is incapable of loving; and therefore purity is an indispensable condition for seeing and apprehending God. The heart is a delicate plant, living upon the drop of dew which falls from heaven; if it be dragged down into the coarseness of earthly things, it will droop like a flower which has been bruised; the flower loses its perfume, the colour fades, and the lifeless stem withers upon the ground. The heart, which is no longer pure, loses the power of loving.

If you have ever believed that impure passion could love you with real love, it was a fearful delusion; for whenever passion exercises its dominion affection soon disappears. The passion of man loves nothing less than the woman who has been weak enough to yield to him. He sees in woman first the gratification of his passion, then weakness, lastly (he will not, indeed, say, but he will think it), he sees in her naught but a thing to be despised.

Nothing is more sure to inspire contempt than the woman who has been weak and sinful. You feel it by the power of a single glance, by the intuitive consciousness of your heart, writhing in its last agony. The end of the indulgence of sinful passion is contempt; man always ends by despising weakness.

It is certain that if the heart is to have any high aspirations, it must be pure, and it must be pure if it is to be loved. What are the hearts we should wish to gather round us in life? Ask yourselves, my sisters, what are the hearts, the hearts in sympathy with your own, whom you would fain have as the companions of your own soul, to walk with you along the road of life, on that path which is called the valley of tears? Would it not be the hearts that have been most pure, the souls most like unto the angels? You would ask for St. John, who was purity itself; for Magdalen, who recovered her innocence by her penitence; for St. Augustine, St. Bernard, St. Teresa, St. Francis of Sales; all these noble hearts, who were so loving only because they were so pure.

Let me observe in passing, that in meditating the other day upon this point, I felt grieved at the manner in which modern society misconstrues the works of those great Christian minds. In these works men now see only weakness and enthusiasm; they are incapable of appreciating the greatness that is in them.

These pages abound with expressions full of generous fervour, the exuberance of pure hearts who lived in the light of divine things. The world, looking only through a prism which deceives and disfigures, sees therein naught but vulgarity and puerility; weakness in that which in reality is real greatness.

When you are no longer pure you lose the appreciation of truth. You instinctively form rash judgments; you see only evil, and that which is good is hidden from you.

The heart cannot love unless it be pure. If it be not pure how should it see God, how should it wing its flight so high? The great power within the heart, whereby it can lift itself up to God, is detachment from earthly things, purity. This is the burden of Holy Scripture. "The net is broken," (so sing the pure in heart), "I may wing my flight and mount up to God."

Naught is so lovely as the pure mind, the pure heart! And this purity may be felt everywhere; in the home, in conjugal life; in the maiden, as beneath the whitened head of the aged woman, a purity which is relative indeed, but a purity which constitutes the depth, the splendour of the soul; it is the rising upwards of the soul to God, the realization of the words of the Gospel: "Blessed are the pure in heart, for they shall see God."

This is the first step in the life of union with God.

But there is a second step, my sisters, for it is not enough to see God. You may see a person, but this does not satisfy you ; you want a nearer, a more intimate relation, you want the spoken word, the conscious glance, the opening lips, something that shall reveal the soul within.

With God, too, there is a second relation. You see Him by purity, you see Him in the world of faith, in the world of the Bible, even through the things of earth. All great minds have seen God through things visible and tangible. I forgot to say that St. Teresa, she whose heart was so simple, so childlike, and whose writings breathe alike the splendour and the delicacy of her intellect, she through the tiny flower beheld God, saying with exquisite tenderness : " It is the smile of God."

St. Francis of Assisi, also, in the midst of his hard and austere life, saw God in all His creatures; the bird flapping its little wings, the fish darting through the stream, all furnished him with an opportunity of rising up to God. The pure in heart always see God.

But I have said, my sisters, it is not enough to see God, we must also speak to Him. We speak to Him in prayer. This honour is conferred upon the soul; it may call God, and ask for an audience of Him. God comes at the soul's call; He draws aside, as it were, the curtain of heaven; He opens out His eternity! He bows His ear, and says: "There in the depths of creation, in the lowest depths of the universe, there is a soul desiring to speak to Me; I hear her!" And the eternal harmonies are hushed, and God listens to this soul as though she were alone in the world.

How great, how incomparable an honour. To call upon God! God bows down to you; you may speak to Him, mount up to Him; you have in your hands this treasure of prayer. Prayer is but the rising up of the soul to God.

But if prayer is to be more than the mere murmur of the lips, more than a passing breath, a vague sigh, a useless, meaningless supplication, the soul must indeed rise up and reach God. Above all, your thoughts in prayer must dwell upon the rights of God, and upon His sovereignty. Your prayers are almost always selfish; you think more of yourselves than of God; you come before Him, ceaselessly pre-occupied with yourselves; and therefore your prayers are cold and icy; you have no idea of His majesty, of His greatness; and therefore your prayers have little reverence; you have no idea of the perfections of God, and therefore in your prayers there is but little recollection. You do not come before Him with the feeling of your own littleness, and the sense of His infinite power. Recollection of spirit is absolutely necessary before God.

You must also be humble in God's presence. Humility is truth; if you are true you must also be humble. To be humble is to see that there is nothing good in us, or that if there is, it is God who gave it to us, and we who have marred it. Humility is to judge oneself truly. If you are just to yourselves, you will have the feeling of your own helplessness, of your own weakness; and your prayer will be the sincere cry of the publican, from the lowest place in the temple: "Be merciful unto me, O God, I am a sinner."

This is the true prayer, the only one which

humanity can utter. All others have been given from heaven by God Himself.

Your romantic phrases, your modern books of devotion, with their pompous periods over which you fall asleep, or dream, these are not prayers; prayer is the earnest, sincere cry of the heart, a cry ever one and the same, one to which God ever listens, "My God, have mercy upon me, for I am a miserable sinner; my soul is miserable." This is the true cry of humanity—humility.

The third feeling is that of confidence. Draw near to God without fear. We are no longer under the law of fear. God is not a tyrant; He is a Sovereign, but He is also a loving Friend—a Brother. Mount, then, up to Him with confidence. What if your heart be chill, your soul cold, your words spiritless; what then! Go to Him with confidence, with a confidence which doubts nothing, with a confidence which *will* be heard. Often you pray without wishing to be heard; you must *will* to be heard. You ask sometimes for your conversion, but it is the last thing you really desire; you want a *compromise*, not a conversion. You ask for the grace of humility; but you do not really wish for it ; you have no real desire to be humble ; you are far too anxious to shine, to be of importance, to be looked up to, to have the petty government of some few other minds, some other hearts. You pray for detachment from the things of this earth ; but at heart you are longing for the fine dresses, the outward display of your friends, of those who, perhaps, make more show than you in the world of fashion. You do not wish to be heard ; you pray not to have your prayers accepted by God, but to obtain a compromise.

Therefore it is that God looks only with pity on your prayers ; He knows that they are not honest, not offered with faith. Well, still you must trust in God: draw near to Him. Cast yourselves at His feet ; He may let you wait for years ; but, as says St. Francis of Sales, " our trust in God must be boundless." In this world every stay is frail: a reed which breaks in the hand. Were you even without any stay, were you left alone as the beggar on the highway, without even eyes wherewith to weep, or hands to stretch forth for the bread of charity ; if (forgive me the supposition) you had not even left to you the poor dumb animal which is the faithful companion of the blind ; if you were forsaken, rejected by all—still could you raise your heart on high, and say those blessed words which are at once the cry of the troubled conscience and the solace of the heart : " Our Father, Who art in heaven."

How comforting is it to feel that in the heights of heaven we have a Father who numbers the hairs of our head, and in the Tabernacle, a Friend who listens to our cry ! Why are you anxious ? Why make your life a perpetual trouble, a continual agitation ! You have heaven, and you can say, " Our Father !" You have the ever-open Church, where you can say, " My brother, my friend !" Why, then, will you go away? Can you not understand these out-pourings of humility, of trust, of fervour ?

It is not enough to speak to God in prayer ; you must be joined to Him by love, that love that makes of the Heart of Jesus and of your own but one heart, by that divine tenderness which binds up your life with the life of God. You must realize within yourselves those words hitherto unknown in the language of men, that saying of the apostle, " It is God, it is Jesus Christ Who liveth in me."

My life is not the life of my troubled, questioning, agitated mind ; not the life of my heart, sad, restless, jealous ; not the life of my darkened, burdened conscience ; not the life of my body, subject as it is to pain ; life is not there, or it is but a cold dim life ; but there is that in me which lives really, lives through love ; it is Jesus Christ, the living God. You know that the soul when under the influence of passion is subjugated by it ; it no longer, as it were, lives its own personal life ; its thoughts are the thoughts of another, the beatings of its heart are the beatings of a heart not its own ; it has a fixed pre-occupation.

Well then, when God enters into a soul, when He takes possession of it, this soul lives by love. Why should we not love God ? Whom should you love ? We ought to love God, first, because He created us ; because He called us into life, and took us by the hand. He created us in His own likeness, He willed that we should be images of Him, reflecting His beauty, His glory. He made Himself in our likeness ; at Bethlehem, He made Himself a little child ; at Nazareth, He chose to bear the sweat of labour and the toil of life; in Judea, He underwent the sorrows of existence in the Garden of Olives, He was borne down by utter loneliness and desolation of heart ; on Calvary, He was scourged, bruised, crucified. He made Himself in our likeness that we might love Him more, for we love those only who are like unto us, who have a common destiny with ourselves. Jesus has loved us passionately, loved us as none other ever has.

This is the one great mystery ; I know of no other ; the others may, in one way or another, be easily grasped by the intellect. There is only one mystery. How to us, the miserable creatures of an hour, whose pale, weakly life is like that of the fading flower, waiting only for the evening hour to die, God yet grants this unspeakable favour ! From the heights of His eternity, He, Who the angels adore, He, Whose robe of stars shines more brilliantly than the brightest gems of earth, God deigns to bow down, and to search amidst the dust of the earth for that small piece of money which we call the human heart ! What then is this heart of ours that Jesus should be jealous of it ? Who is jealous of your heart in the world? In your family, you meet but with passing affections; a few years and you are betrayed, earlier still perhaps despised. No one asks for your heart here below, God alone asks for it! You have a price to pay for the earthly love which fascinates and pursues you; and think you that God's love exacts nothing? If you reject the love of God, He will take vengeance, for love that is abused ever avenges itself, and the vengeance of God is His justice.

My sisters, draw near to God by faith, by prayer, by love. Go to Him trustingly, whatever be the state of your soul. Even if the deep emotions awakened within you during this retreat should be insufficient, and you still hesitate to give your-selves wholly to God, yet when the supreme hour comes, send forth one last cry to Him, and He will accept you; one word from out of the depths of your soul is enough; He is waiting for you. I will conclude by reminding you of a touching incident recorded in the gospels.

A woman had heard of Jesus Christ, of His goodness, His gentleness, His miracles; she seeks to draw near to Him; she has a favour to ask of Him; although a stranger, yet she comes, she beseeches Him. The Master shrouds Himself under an apparent severity; He veils the tenderness of His aspect, His look becomes stern; He says to her, "Thou seekest a miracle; it is not right to take the children's bread, and to give it to dogs."

My sisters, has God ever given you such an answer as this? He has been silent, perhaps, but He has never answered you thus.

The poor Canaanite woman is not discouraged; she falls upon her knees, bowing down and trembling she exclaims in words of ineffable pathos, "True, Lord, I am not worthy to receive the bread which is on the table, but the dogs eat the crumbs which fall from their master's table; give me of the crumbs of Thy table."

The Master beheld her, it was this trusting answer He had waited for; and He answers, "O woman, great is thy faith; be it unto thee according as thou hast said."

And in that same hour her daughter was healed.

My sisters, let the Canaanite's trust be yours,

To-morrow, you are coming to the holy Table to receive, not material bread, the bread which is of the earth, but the Bread of Heaven. Hardly are you worthy of the crumbs from the Table of Jesus Christ; but learn to draw near to Him in faith; pour forth the trusting cry of prayer, of love; and He will receive you as He did the poor woman of Canaan. You will then see that it is better to be united to God than to the world, for you will find in Jesus the Word, which gives light, the Heart, which comforts, and the Power, which alone can bless you in this world and the next.

The Life of Self-devotion.

"Quandiù fecistis uni ex hei fratribus meis minimis, mihi fecistis"—"As long as you did it to one of these my least brethren, you did it to me."—St. Matthew xxv. 40.

E have now, my sisters, nearly reached the end of our retreat, let us then cast a retrospective glance over all that I have been saying to you, and make a general review of the principles which I have developed in our meditations.

The fundamental idea was that in the original divine scheme, God created you for His glory. The great end of creation is the glory of God; this, then, should be the one aim of every exercise of your intellect, of every action of your life; God must dwell within you, His Spirit must abide in your hearts.

I told you also that there were obstacles to this supernatural life, and that they were many. The first is, that spirit of personality, that self-love which insinuates itself into the soul and pervades the whole course of your existence. You have seen how this exaggerated idea of your own value brings with it disquietude, agitation, and uncertainty of mind. I am alluding to the feeling which makes us wish to exercise a dominion over all that surrounds us, to tyrannize over others, thus making self the one centre to which we would fain that all things should radiate so that self alone may receive glorification and honour.

The second obstacle is the spirit of the world. I have shown ·you that in the world you will find neither the ideal which you seek, nor the support which you require in your duties, in your dangers, in your sorrows ; neither will you find that affection for which your heart craves. All the habits and the opinions of this world are essentially opposed to Christianity; I have said too, with what prudence and circumspection you ought to go into the world.

The third obstacle is the evil spirit, the tempter.

15

I have shown you the existence of the tempter; how he places himself in communication with every living being, holding converse with each soul, with each individual intellect, drawing near to every woman as he drew near to Eve in the terrestrial paradise, and to our Lord Jesus in the desert; how he is in fact the tempter, the cause of all spiritual ruin and devastation, leading from temptation to the fall, from the fall to despair.

I have told you that the remedy against these three evil spirits, self, the world, and the devil, is the life of faith, the clear comprehension of supernatural truth, a life of sacrifice, of self-immolation, of mortification, of self-crucifixion. I assured you that such a life, far from being one of sadness and misery, was in fact the only truly happy one. Supernatural life alone can give happiness.

I said this morning that the soul becomes united to God by the purity which enables it to behold Him, by the heart which is lifted up to Him, by the conscience which loves Him. Union with God is the ascent of the soul to the vision of God by purity and by prayer until it attains to a perfect and intimate communion with Him.

The one thing needful is to strive to live with God.

I know not if you have ever thought of one of the mysteries of Christianity, which to us is one of the profoundest mysteries of our faith. The priest has the incomparable joy, the indescribable happiness, of ascending every day to the holy altar with the firm belief both in his heart and conscience that he will then come in immediate contact with his God!

A Protestant once said to me, "I cannot believe in the Eucharist."

I answered, "And yet it is a truth established by divine teaching, by the testimony of the Gospels, by the virtues which flourish in the world."

" I cannot believe it."

" Why ?"

" Because, after ascending to the altar, you can re-descend to the earth. I cannot understand how, after holding every morning half an hour's converse with God, you can still hold converse with men."

And this is true.

Just as Moses, when he came down from Mount Sinai, where he had been holding converse with God, found the Israelites gathered around the golden calf; so the priest, after having in the morning ascended to the resplendent summit of Mount Thabor and assisted at the divine mystery of the Transfiguration, is forced to descend the mountain of this life into the low valleys of the earth, where men in their sordid ingratitude cease not to crowd around the golden calf—I mean minds engrossed and absorbed by all the pettinesses, the vulgarities, the sensualities of life.

And herein is a mystery! When God has given Himself to us, He requires that we should share Him with others. We are not to be selfish possessors of our faith and of His blessings and love; the treasure of grace and of eternal truth is not to be hidden wealth.

Therefore it is that whenever a soul has found God, whenever she has entered into real communion with Him, and that He has become her food and her life, she feels the desire of giving Him to others, of communicating Him to those who have Him not. The soul where God dwells is like the sun, which cannot contain his rays, but throws them out in burning darts.

The soul praying in the obscurity of the cloister, the humble maiden shrouded in her habit of serge —the poor Clare, or the Carmelite—she makes God known unto men, by her prayers and meditations if not by her actions. It would seem that souls such as these exhale a sweet dew, which, rising to heaven, falls down again on the earth in blessings for others.

During this retreat, it is not what I have said which has touched you, and given you the desire of giving yourselves more entirely unto God ; it is, my sisters, that in this city there are those who, in the solitude and silence of their cloisters, have prayed that my words might be blessed. Oh, if with the eyes of faith you could but see the blessings which may be gained by prayer ! blessings which, falling upon our poor earth, scorched and parched up as it is by the flames of worldliness, restore to it some degree of life, of freshness, and of bloom.

Such is the power of those souls who, by prayer, by devotion, by self-sacrifice, and self-immolation,

have attained unto the possession of God. It is
like unto the grain of incense, which, thrown into
the censer, re-descends, like a perfumed cloud, on
the crowd below!

Modern society has no comprehension of the
contemplative life; it can only understand action
—exterior devotion.

What I chiefly recommend to you as the best
means of doing good to those around you is to
withdraw into solitude, and to pray to God.

You trust in your power of activity, in the influence of your feminine strategy. Not therein
lies your strength; your strength is in prayer.
You are anxious about your children; a cloud
passes over your heart respecting your husband's
affection; you are sad, desponding, spiritless. Go,
and kiss the feet of your crucifix. Pray—ask God
to bless you, and then return to the bosom of your
family, to your domestic life; and great will be
your power!

A great minister, the illustrious Cardinal Ximenès,
that once poor monk (whom the wind of fortune,
or, rather, the will of Providence, dragged out of an
obscure cell, and placed on the heights of social

life, that he might thence rule over a great nation), had one day made an appointment in his palace with the grandees of the kingdom. They were all assembled, expecting him, talking together, and complaining that they were kept waiting. Suddenly, the Cardinal opened the door of the room which he had just left—a monastic cell, which, in the midst of all the splendours around him, he had reserved for himself—"You are impatient," he said, with dignity, to his assembled guests. "I was at the foot of my crucifix; remember that to pray is still to govern."

And this, my sisters, is the one thing which I would impress upon you for the government of your families and for the direction of your whole life in the world. To pray is to govern. Did you but know how to rule by prayer, you would do so far more than by your words; you would govern by the power of God, and not by your own.

I must now speak to you of other kinds of self-devotion. I will not dwell on the necessity of self-sacrifice; I should do injustice both to your own nature and to your heart. Suffering and self-sacrifice are essentially your portion. You sometimes imagine yourselves to be created for pleasure and enjoyment. It is an illusion. Woman is created only for suffering and self-sacrifice. As long as you do not understand this great end of your life, of your whole destiny, you will perhaps complain of your place in the order of creation. Yet you need not lament; for is not your fellowship, of all others, the highest, the most sublime—even with Jesus Christ Himself—with Him, Who is essentially " the man of sorrows, acquainted with grief."

I have said that suffering is your portion, because there is within you a greater power of suffering than in man. Man does not know how to endure suffering. When he is in pain, however slight, however transient, he is overpowered by it, he needs help and protection. He cannot bear sorrow. If there is a coffin in the house, the man is restless. He goes to his business, to his politics, to his books, or to his amusements—anything to distract his mind. The woman, on the contrary, can remain in her home silent and alone, face to face with her grief and its memories, tortured in mind, broken down in body, but still strong to endure. Men cannot bear suffering, and therefore do they need that God should grant them more exemption from suffering than women.

Moreover, my sisters, you have within you far more of the spirit of self-devotion than men. I do not wish to calumniate men, but I must allow that the affection of a man is never thoroughly perfect and disinterested ; it is almost always selfish. With a woman this is more rare ; she is essentially self-devoted, because she was created only to be man's companion, his helpmate, and his joy. Man suffices to himself ; he has the majesty of his own sovereignty. Woman is obliged to lean on man for her support. It would seem as if she had been created both to receive and to give support. Self-devotion is part of her nature.

Two years ago I quoted to you these words of a saint : " Man is a being who must love ; woman is essentially a being who has a heart to give."

Such is your life, my sisters. You only ask to give yourselves to another. To feel yourselves alone, with none near you to claim any share of your heart ; this is for you the great sorrow of life, shaking the foundations of your soul, of your very being.

When, as young girls, you feel yourselves isolated in life; when, in your widowhood, you have no one on whom you can lean, no one who cares for your affection; when separated, perhaps, from your family, you halt wearily on your road through life, and exclaim, "No one needs me! Oh, believe me, the greatest misery would be preferable to such loneliness!" you have then to face life's greatest trial, weariness, lassitude, oppression of heart.

Your nature, then, is essentially formed for companionship, for self-devotion. Does not this prove it? But this self-devotion must be inspired by Jesus Christ Himself, and not be the mere impulse of caprice or of sympathy. When you are fond of any one, you would throw the whole world at their feet; but if you dislike them, how quick you then are in finding out their secret failings, in exposing their infirmities, and casting a slur on their characters! You are influenced only by your sympathies or your antipathies. Yet surely these ought not to be the real causes of your self-devotion.

Your nature requires action; but you waste your energies on outside things. You are afraid to be

face to face with your own selves; you act fever-
ishly, breathlessly. That is not self-devotion.

Sometimes you take up an affection only as a
distraction, and because you are a burthen to yourselves.

Again, your self-devotion must not be ostenta-
tious, like the Pharisee, who sounds the trumpet
and gives his alms in public, saying, "I am not as
other men are."

Neither must it be a means of escape from the
calls of domestic life. Some people throw themselves into a sort of feverish activity of self-devotion
in order to exempt themselves from their more
immediate duties. The consequence is that they
fail in kindness, in unselfishness, in the accomplishment of their primary obligations; they change
the order of God's Providence. How many women
will be found guilty because they have neglected
to make good Christians of their husbands!

When all that was required was a little kindness,
a little affection, a certain tact in self-devotion,
which would have been thoroughly appreciated,
how many women, instead of trying to raise the
minds, to elevate the feelings of their husbands,

have had no higher aim than that of making them the instruments of their own caprices!

We read of St. Elizabeth of Hungary, that when her husband went away she put on mourning, but that when he returned she dressed herself in gay apparel. Things are somewhat rather changed since the days of St. Elizabeth! When your husbands go away, you are tempted to put on your best clothes, and when they come back you would often, I think, feel inclined to go into mourning! The result is, that he is often like a stranger in his own house—like a guest at an inn. There is no domestic intimacy. You are as strangers one to another. There is no conversation about the future of the children, no community of prayer, of duties, of hopes. You do not know how to influence your husbands; and yet they, surely, should be the first objects of your love and self-devotion.

It is all very well, no doubt, to busy yourselves with the salvation of Chinese children; to dry the tears of unhappy Poland; to tend incurables. But before the Chinese child, before the destitute foreigner, before the sick of the hospital, your husband has a right to your loving care.

It is certain that in our own days there are wonderful illusions about the manner of fulfilling Christian duties. What is the cause of this? I know
not whether it springs from a want of faith, or from
the want of the spirit of self-sacrifice; but it is
positive that therein lies a great peril, and that at
the hour of death many souls will see their errors
with horror. For it is simply a want of comprehension of the first duty of life. You might have
done good to souls who would thus have ascended the
ladder of perfection. By reading together, working
together, mutually strengthening each other, good
and holy thoughts and desires are exchanged and
communicated. Other men are like your husband ;
only you see them through a sympathetic prism ;
whereas your own husband is viewed by the light
of the antipathy which arises out of the difficult
position in which you are both placed, and of
which the bitterness of your own temper is perhaps
the real cause. If you would but bring the whole
strength of your will to bear on this difficulty, you
would fulfil a real mission.

You see, therefore, that your self-devotion must
first be exercised in your own homes.

You must also devote yourselves to your children. You must be full of kindness, full of real Christian feeling towards them. You must not think only of their earthly career; you must not lose sight of their life above, of their heavenward road; you must bring them up in the grand hope of eternal life. Train their young minds so that they may one day become really great; remember whatever was faulty in your own education, and correct it in them. Do not allow mercenary influences alone to direct the first years of those lives which are so dear to you. Let these little beings begin their existence under the eye of their mother, so that thus, initiated by you into the beauties of religion, and instructed later on by Christian teaching in their own homes, they may become possessors of the great treasures of eternity. Such ought to be your self-devotion at home and in your own families.

I am often asked, my sisters, to preach charity sermons; not only at Lyons, but in Paris, at Bordeaux, everywhere. Well, whenever this happens; whenever they apply to me for a sermon; I begin by preaching to them charity at home, in their own families, towards their own relations. For, in point of fact, Christian women are very like worldly women, and worldly women like Christian women. Worldly women make use of society in order to escape from their husbands; Christian women make use of church or sacristy work as an excuse to escape from their domestic duties.

The first object of your self-devotedness should ever be in your own homes.

Self-devotion should not, however, stop here. You are favoured by God in your birth; your social position; by the comforts with which you are surrounded; by the blessings He has bestowed upon you. You do not think enough of thanking Him for these things; you do not forget enough your own little troubles, the pin-pricks of life! You do not sufficiently look around you. You do not penetrate into those streets where the great masses of the population are heaped up together, where live poor sickly women, deprived, perhaps, of the light of the sun, and condemned to hard and laborious work in order to earn daily bread for themselves and their children; poor, half-starved creatures, with helpless infants hanging on their breasts, little new-born babes, who in vain seek the food which their mothers cannot give them. And these poor creatures live on day after day, struggling, suffering, and when at night, worn out and wearied, they return to their homes, their only welcome is too often the brutality of their husbands, whose iron hands seem to crush them as easily as you may crush a tender plant.

And yet these are women, with the natures of women. In the lowest grades of society may be found refined and delicate natures. They may, perhaps, be less sensitive than you ; and yet sometimes, when these poor women have opened their hearts to me, I have found some amongst them possessing all the delicacy and refinement of the most educated classes. And yet these, too, were forced to earn their daily bread, painfully, laboriously ; their lot was that of perpetual suffering, perpetual abnegation.

Ah ! my sisters, you do not sufficiently thank God for the blessings with which He has loaded you. You have had little troubles, perhaps, on your road, but you forget what real, what cruel sorrow there is round about you.

God has placed you in your present position in order that you may dispense some of your superfluity to those who need it. Give alms, then. Give them yourselves; but do not give them in a contemptuous manner. Because you are superior in fortune, do not, therefore, look down on those whom you assist. The first essential in self-devotion is to love those to whom the devotion is given. If you cannot love the poor because they are in themselves lovable, love them in Jesus Christ. Forget their exterior, which fills you with aversion, the rags which disgust, the vices which horrify you. Look beyond, into their souls, and do homage to the Divine image of Jesus Christ which you may there find.

Oh, what power may such self-devotion give you! A poetical writer once said: "In order to govern the souls of men, you must love them." Love, then, those to whom you strive to do good.

One of you observed to me that it was impossible to do any good unless the heart gave its co-operation. You must, then, devote yourselves to the poor, through motives of love, tenderness, and charity.

How is it that the poor man may sometimes be seen lifting up his eyes to heaven ? It is a subject on which I love to dwell again and again when I am preaching. When a poor man finds himself out of work, when he is obliged to beg for bread for the support of his family ; when wandering about the streets deserted and abandoned, he writhes under the pressure of his misery, then is he sometimes tempted to blaspheme and to cry : " Why is it that so many have riches and fortune, whilst others are dying of hunger ?"

But, then, one day there comes to this poor man a little sister of the poor, or a sister of charity, and she says to him : " God has not abandoned you, for He sends me to you ; I left my father and mother, all the comforts and the joys of home; I left fortune and luxury, I gave up everything in order that I might become your sister out of love and charity ; in order that I might take you by the hand and help you along your hard and rugged path ; no, you are not deserted, not friendless."

And when the sister, with her sweet smile, has thus spoken to him, when at last she takes hold of his hand, then the poor man's heart is touched, however hardened by misery. His very soul is moved, he looks up to heaven, tears roll down his cheeks, and with a smile on his lips he exclaims: " I will no longer blaspheme. I have a Father in heaven. I know it now, since I have found a sister on earth."

Thus does charity show him providence; love teaches him to see his God, and all this is revealed to him by the sister's life of purity and self-devotion.

The first condition, then, of self-devotion, from the point of view of faith, is to love; not to treat the poor disdainfully, but to make them feel as if you were one of themselves. It is a great thing for you that God should thus have associated you in the designs of His providence; but it is a greater thing still that you should be called to minister to Jesus Christ Himself.

The poor man is Jesus Christ; you, the rich, only take the place of providence when you assist him. Beneath the rags of the poor beggar, or the squalid misery of the little orphan girl; beneath all the sufferings of the incurables, and of the wretched ones of the earth, underlying all your good works with their manifest fruits, you ought ever to see Jesus Christ. Real self-devotion is, therefore, founded on supernatural love. Kindled by this sacred flame, it burns brighter near the tabernacle, and is nourished by the blood of Jesus Christ.

The second condition is that your self-devotion should be persevering.

I have said that by nature you have but little stability. One of the elements of your feminine nature is that you are impatient; you will not wait, you are anxious for a result, for success. When you do good to any one, you think there must be an immediate transformation. You visit poor people, you nurse the sick, you look after old women; the moment you see no immediate effect you are discouraged, and you complain.

Are we so successful with you, my sisters? When that sick nurse of humanity, the confessor, sits waiting for you to go to him, week by week, month by month, or, it may be, year by year, when he has to wait until it shall please you to pour out to him the contents of your hearts, do you not see therein God's mercy and indulgence which thus patiently awaits your conversion twenty, thirty years, more even sometimes? And this holy patience of God, can you not imitate it with the souls with whom you have to deal?

Be persevering, therefore; but for this you must learn to govern yourselves; perseverance is the fruit of personal discipline, of bearing with oneself; you will only learn to bear with others when you have learnt to bear with yourselves. To bear with others is the chief feature of self-devotion. To bear with those about us, to maintain that evenness of temper, that kindliness of heart, that cheerfulness and serenity which so greatly enhance all acts of kindness. This sweetness, this transfiguration of the heart by Jesus Christ possesses in itself a wonderful power! It is, in fact, that perseverance which will not allow itself to be discouraged, which is happy because it is blessed with a divine benediction.

Devote yourselves, then, my sisters, lovingly and perseveringly to those around you.

And to whom ought you to devote yourselves? I repeat it, first to those in your own home; then to all who suffer, to all who weep, to all who here below are in sorrow and need.

There is a passage in Holy Writ which is magnificent in its truth, and which is at the same time a sublime eulogy on you: " Where woman is not, there the poor and the sick languish"—" *Ubi non est mulier, ingemiscit egens.*"

It would seem as if it were impossible to solace sorrow and woe if woman be not at hand. Therefore it is that in that sublime picture which is the perpetual representation of the source of all consolation and strength for the human race, there was but one man but many women. There were the tears of a poor woman falling upon the feet of Jesus, there, also, was the mother of consolation.

There exists in woman a great power of consolation.

Every sorrow belongs to you, all suffering is in your dominion ; you have but one province, the province of consolation, the rulership (if I may so say) over sorrow.

Wherever, then, you find a suffering soul, a sad heart, a wounded conscience, a child in want of bread, a poor man out of work, a soul longing to regain her purity, there ought you to go. Therefore it is that we give you distant missions amongst those who are the most desolate, that we, as bishops, wish to enlist you as collectors for our churches ; that we make you into missionaries and apostles. Your ear should be ever open to hear the cry of suffering; to bind up the broken-hearted, and in so doing you will find your real treasure, your true consolation.

A Christian woman is, indeed, a grand creation of the Catholic Church !

And when in my weary fights with heresy I wish to prove to some poor, incredulous souls the grandeur of the Catholic Church, instead of demonstrating this (as of course I might have done) by doctrinal and controversial explanations, I always prefer to direct attention to the Christian woman (and this proof is unanswerable). I point to her in her educational mission in the cloister, or again in the world, fulfilling her duties cheerfully and sweetly, seeking no glory for herself, but bearing her husband's name honoured and unsullied, the happiness of her children, the blessing of her family ; the woman who, clothed in her self-devotion and in her supernatural virtue, thinks nothing of leaving the splendours of life to go and console those who suffer, those who weep. I cited, also, the example of those poor workwomen of whom I spoke just now ; of those simple-hearted girls who make their humble offerings, either for Peter's pence, for the missions, or for other good works ; caring but for one thing, the propagation of the faith, asking only whether the standard of God is advancing in the world.

In conclusion, you must devote yourselves, my sisters, to whatsoever suffers and mourns here below. Therefore, also, you owe a portion of your self-devotion to the holy Church of God, to that good mother who is often in tears and in mourning. I would I could make you truly love the Church. You only respect and love her for the sake of the halo of Mary Immaculate with which she has encircled your brow, casting on it the reflection of a glory which may be said to have in it something which is both virginal and maternal. You ought to weep over her defeats, rejoice at her triumphs, take part in her joys ; you must be faithful to her, you must love and salute her as a bride and as a queen.

You must also devote yourselves to our Lord, the

Prisoner in the tabernacle, the Abandoned, the for-saken One. In some tabernacles He is destitute of covering; the poverty of churches in the country is often extreme. Strive to remedy this.

You must devote yourselves to God, Who is ever seeking for souls; you must devote yourselves because there are souls who are empty, dying; hearts without God, consciences going to ruin.

Is not this truly a field for your apostolate, my sisters? And you will exercise it by your faith, by your generosity, by the infusion of divine life into the souls of others; thus giving them the one great help which they need for eternity.

And in what manner can you devote yourselves? First by your words.

I might speak to you of the conversations among young girls who are already anticipating the future, and know already how to make themselves familiar with the dangers and the allurements of the world; of certain confidential conversations in which young women ought not to indulge; of the conversations of women more advanced in age, in which the sensualities and the intrigues of the world are recalled to the memory; of the sinful conversations of women with each other or with men ; but this would take a whole chapter, for I should have much to say.   I pass it by, therefore ; but remember that a woman's words can be so powerful that they may become as the seed which shall bear fruit an hundredfold.

A single word said with faith, with simplicity, with kindness, and with sweetness may, if it fall upon a suffering soul, open out to that soul the way to heaven and cause God to descend within it.

I will add, but without developing the thought, that you may also make your life, your whole existence, your fortune, all that you possess, the means of self-devotion.

My sisters, I will leave these reflections with you. Prepare yourself to receive the source, the essence of eternal self-devotion.   That which inspires and gives strength to the priest, which clothes the maiden with her robe of purity, gives to woman the courage of virtue, and to the aged Christian hope and calm resignation in death.   Prepare yourselves to receive it.

I will end by suggesting to you an idea which may be made into a fruitful source of self-devotion.

I quote the words of a woman, who, crushed by a great sorrow, took refuge in a convent, where she is now happy in her cell : " I learnt," she said, " but too late, that for woman there is but one real sorrow and one real happiness; the sorrow of having offended God ; the happiness of being a child of holy Church."

"Blessed are they who hear the word of God and keep it."

MY sisters, you have had the happiness of hearing the word of God. The divine Master has addressed Himself to your souls ; He has revealed to you your struggles, your infirmities, your falls, your sorrows, your mission, your apostolate, your duties, and, at the same time, the glorious destiny promised to you. Great light has been given to you by this divine word, it has taught you a deeper knowledge of God, a deeper knowledge of your own selves.

You have learnt to understand the fervent exclamation of St. Augustin : " My God, grant that I may know Thee, that I may know myself!" And in thus learning to know God you have felt that you may not waste the treasures of your heart, the riches of your mind, the best feelings of your life, the powers of your imagination, on the futilities of the world, but that you must direct them heavenwards unto God.

With this fresh knowledge of yourselves you have learnt how you should mistrust your own strength or rather your own weakness; you have learnt the greatness of the perils that surround you, and how everywhere, even in your own homes, you are met by the great conflicts and sorrows of life.

But if I contented myself with showing you your own shortcomings, your difficulties, and your infirmities, with reminding you of your tears and your sorrows, my ministry would be but a barren and a comfortless one; only one thing would be left for you to do; you could but sit down helplessly and mourn over your own ruin and desolation; but, my sisters, the word of God must have its completion. This word you will doubtless retain within you; the remembrance of it will be sweet and pleasant to you; but I repeat, it requires a completion, it needs an ending, a crowning something which shall be more consoling, more satisfying to your heart; this completion is the eternal Word, the uncreated Word, the life eternal God, Who deigns to come and dwell within you.

You feel this in your very innermost being; while in heaven there is joy incomparable; and the earth rejoices, also, because of the souls that are returning to Jesus Christ.

You are going to receive our Lord! Is it a reality, or is it not a dream? Is it a real presence, or is it but a symbol? Is it a life, or is it nothing but a remembrance or a hope?

My sisters, our Lord is there, in all His divine truth, in all the reality of His substantial presence, of His presence affirmed by His words, and by His spouse the Church; He is there, for He has said: "He who eateth My flesh and drinketh My blood hath life, whosoever eateth not My flesh, nor drinketh My blood is dead."

It is He, too, Who said: "This is My body, take and eat. This is My blood, take and drink."

And He added: "I am the living Bread that came down from heaven."

He is present, therefore, and for the last nineteen centuries has the Church been on her knees before Him, in trembling admiration and wondering love;

angels bend down before the tabernacle ; priests in their white sacerdotal vestments distribute the sacred bread. Jesus Christ is therefore present.

But in order that He may enter into your souls a great operation is necessary. Jesus Christ dwells in three tabernacles of which your own hearts must in a manner become the image.

His first tabernacle is His Mother. His Mother ! She is immaculate and beautiful with a transcendant beauty ; but in order that she may be worthy to bear Him for months within her womb, it is necessary that God should mould her from all eternity, that He should make her immaculate in her conception, pure in her birth, spotless in her life, glorious in her death and in her assumption. And because she was thus preserved like a pure white lily, may she receive into her womb this heavenly Pearl, the purity of the Sun of Justice.

The second tabernacle is in heaven ; since the very origin of all things God has sat on His throne in the splendour of His glory, illuminating with His divine rays the eternal city, pouring forth on all souls treasures of immeasurable love. Of His substance are the elect nourished, angels bow down before Him, singing an eternal *alleluia ;* the ancients swing their censers laden with perfume. The tabernacle of heaven is one of perpetual purity and love.

There is a third tabernacle. God makes use of the hands of man to hew the stone, to build up the arches, to set up an altar whereon to place His tabernacle ; and here, also, do we find purity and love, for this edifice must be consecrated by the bishop, holy oil must be poured upon it, the altar where all that is earthly is to immolate itself, must be surrounded by silence and peace, it must shine with light and be adorned with white ornaments ; there must be gold, that which gives brightness to life in the interior of the ciborium where Jesus dwells. Within the tabernacle, therefore, is also love and purity. In the tabernacle of heaven there is purity and love. In Mary, who is also a tabernacle, there is purity and love. You see, then, how God loves to dwell in purity and love.

My sisters, is your heart, which is about to become a tabernacle to receive your Lord, sufficiently prepared ?

Is it the abode of purity and tenderness, of goodness, of self-devotion, of light and love ? Yes, for you have disciplined it in the silence of retreat; you have nourished yourselves with the holy word of God, you have come in contact with His precious Blood, you have drawn near to the sacred Heart of Jesus by the courage of confession, by the avowal of your faults, by the laborious work of penance, by the sighings of the pure of heart, by the tears from your eyes united with the Blood of Redemption; thus have you purified your souls. And to this purity you have added love. You hunger and thirst for Jesus; you cry: "Oh! when cometh the moment when I shall receive Him?" You call Him with every voice of your soul, and you repeat with the prophets: "God, make us see the just!"

There dwell therefore within you purity and love. Jesus has spoken: this incomparable act, the grandest, the noblest, which human language can describe—this act of Communion, is about to be accomplished in you. God is the life of the world. The body lives upon matter, the mind on the intellectual, the heart on affection, the conscience on purity. But the soul, on what shall it feed? What shall nourish it? Where shall it find its strength, its treasure, its life? In Jesus alone. The soul must find her nourishment in God; she comes from Him, He is her source; she returns to Him, He is her end; the first page in her life is God, the last is still God; in the intermediate pages of her existence, must He still be her sustenance. She must consume her God and live on Him, she must find in Him her delight, so that she may exclaim, "It is God Who is about to come into me as my food; my nourishment is Emmanuel, it is Jesus Himself who said, 'Take, eat, this is My body; take and drink, this is My blood; if ye do not eat My flesh and drink My blood, you have no life in you.'"

Our life, our only life is Jesus, we have no other. Humanity can but give us a mortal life; the earth naught but a fragile and an ephemeral life: the things here below offer us but an uncertain life. There is but one eternal life; it is Jesus coming to dwell in our hearts.

My sisters, come unto Jesus Christ in purity and in love, come to Him in faith; bow down before your God in the tabernacle; tell Him that you believe in Him, in spite of the revolt of your senses, in spite of the doubts of your reason, in spite of the questionings of your intellect. Say, not as the inhabitants of Capernium did: " How can He give His flesh to eat ?"

Jesus would answer: " Verily I say unto you, unless ye eat the flesh of the Son of Man and drink His blood, ye have no life in you."

You must believe in this affirmation, which Jesus has confirmed by an oath ; you must bow down before it with an entire conviction of soul. Come unto Jesus in humility of heart. " My Father," said the Saviour, " I thank Thee that Thou hast hid these things " . . . . what things ? The beauties of heaven ? . . . no—" that Thou hast hid them from the great, and revealed them to the simple and the lowly."

" My Father, I thank Thee."

Be then simple and lowly, my sisters ; simple in heart, lowly in your own eyes ; humbled, subdued, detached from your own selves ; humble yourselves ; come in humility.

One day the Master heard that purest amongst the sons of men, that austere prophet of the desert, the very personification of innocence and purity,

St. John the Baptist, say to Him, "I am not worthy to unloose the latchets of Thy shoes."

But a moment ago, after having received the sacerdotal vestments with which I was to clothe myself, and asked of God that these vestments might preserve my soul from the stains of earth, and be unto me as a bulwark of purity, I made my confession to the priest of God at my side, I beat my breast and confessed to heaven, to angels, and to earth, "It is my fault, my fault, pray for me." Then going up to the altar, I multiplied my ablutions, and again and again washed my hands ; seeking thus external as well as internal purity, and after these successive ablutions, I again beat my breast and cried, "My God, have mercy on me !"

Do not say, my sisters, that you are not worthy of God ; for who is worthy of Him ? All we can do is to strive to be as little unworthy of Him as we can.

Come unto Jesus with confidence because He is the eternal Friend of those who are in sorrow, the eternal Purity of the guilty, the eternal Beauty of the soul stained by sin, the eternal Reward of those who are struggling with temptation, the eternal Affection of those with whom all other affections have failed, the eternal Consolation of those who reject the consolations of this world. Come unto Him, be not afraid ; He is ever the Child of Bethlehem, the Victim of Mount Calvary, the Transfigured One on Mount Thabor, the Life, the Breath of the tabernacle. Draw near with confidence ; be not afraid.

Come especially with love ; bring Him all the treasures of your heart, give Him all your affections. When He shall have passed out of my hands on to your lips, and from your lips into your heart, bow down, adore Him in silence, listen to Him, speak to Him. You will become the tabernacle of the Virgin Mary, the tabernacle of heaven, the tabernacle of the Church, you will be surrounded by angels, reverent and adoring. You will meditate on Him in the depths of your conscience, in the silence of your heart. After having worshipped Him on this altar, you will hear Mass again with Him, you will, so to say, become priests ; you will pray to Him, you will do Him homage, as to the Creator, the Master of the universe ; you will proclaim His rights and His sovereignty; you will thank Him for His mercies; you will beg for grace and you will obtain all that you ask.

After having adored and thanked Him, after having offered yourselves to Him as a grain of incense, after having consumed yourselves like the lights on the altar, you will say, "Lord, make of me a living soul, a soul which shall no more die!" You will confide to Him your weaknesses, the ruling sin of your life, the chief sorrows of your existence; you will seek counsel of Him, respecting all things in which you need light and strength, in all things necessary for you in life. He will hear you; He will divine you, He will understand you. How often you have longed for a heart that should understand your own. He will reveal to you all your infirmities, your struggles, your sorrows, your blessings.

You will speak to Him also of your family, of your children, of your anxieties and your fears for them, of all that makes the joy and the surroundings of your life; even perhaps of some to whom you have given scandal, to whom you may have been the stumbling-block, the occasion of falling.

You will intercede with Him for all whom you ought to love, and to save.

You will speak to Him with confidence and love, praying for the riches of His blessing upon all.

You will plead with Him also for the whole Church, for the sovereign pontiff, for the episcopate, for the priesthood; you will ask of Him that truth may conquer, that Christianity may triumph.

You will pray also for me that I may be the apostle of our faith, that I may have the joy of bringing souls out of darkness into light. You will pray in faith and love, we shall be united in prayer, as we are in friendship; Jesus Christ is the sweet and loving bond between soul and soul. Let us therefore unite in loving and adoring Him; let us pray to Him and give Him thanks, so shall we be associated with the angels of God, we shall form a crown of glory around Him, and honour His holy Name in a canticle of praise.

I shall repeat to Jesus Christ what I said to Him but just now when at my behest He deigned to come down from heaven. Then was it that in the fulness of episcopal power I lifted up my soul to heaven, and the curtains of eternity being withdrawn, I dared to look up to the eternal altar and call down the divine Word; then taking It in my hands and returning to the earth where you were bowed down in adoration, I exclaimed, as I held up the sacred chalice, "O precious Blood of Jesus Christ! O Heart of my God! let Thy blessing descend upon these souls; they have been touched, aroused during this retreat; there are struggles, I know, in the depths of their hearts, there are tears and conflicts; oh! strengthen them in their struggles, comfort them when they weep, pardon wherever there remain the stains of sin; help and pity them in their weakness. Oh! bless these souls, Lord Jesus, that they may be able to keep the eternal Word, that they may lay hold of Thee, and return to the world full of life and of Thee."

Come then, my sisters, come to your transfiguration; soon you will return to your Garden of Olives; when Jesus Christ has come within you, then, with your heart like a living chalice, a spiritual altar, a burning tabernacle, you once more shall go out into the world. After having received Jesus Christ, there is nothing greater then to give Him; come then and receive Him that you may give Him to those you love; all that Jesus Christ now asks of you is faith, humility, confidence, and love; He asks for your heart; give it to Him, He brings you His own.

The Valiant Woman.—The Virgin Mary.

"Mulierem fortem quis inveniet?"—"Who shall find the valiant woman?"

MY sisters, if you have reflected on the fundamental idea in the different meditations which we have made together this week, you must have seen what our Lord especially demands of you is a co-operation in the divine aim for which God has given you life. I said that you were created to glorify God; your aim is His glory; your destiny, His honour. And when we studied the obstacles which you might meet with in your endeavours to attain to this end, we found that they were your weakness, your self-love, the exaggeration of your own personality, the spirit of worldliness, the thousand futilities of life, the thousand trivialities with which you are surrounded. I told you also that besides your own selves, and besides the world, there was the evil spirit, the tempter ; I depicted to you his prodigious hatred of virtue, of truth, of all that is good ; I added that sooner or later the tempter drew nigh to every soul as he drew near to Eve amidst the joys of Eden, and to our great Master in the loneliness of the desert. I said that you might overcome this three-fold obstacle, not by a vague sentimentality, not by an exaggerated piety, not by a sort of parade religion, made up of religious observances, but by a strong conviction, based on reason, and especially by the intelligent comprehension of the great truths of religion, of that which I have called the super-natural life within you ; a life better than your mere human life ; a higher life than your terrestrial life ; you must have the conviction of faith, a firm faith, a faith which propagates itself, a faith which shines on all around you.

I told you also that in order to overcome the obstacles sacrifice was necessary. It is only by sacrifice that you can erect or construct anything in the world ; the law which rules your life is the law of sacrifice. In the Church, there is but one action, the sacrifice of the Mass, the immolation of the eternal victim. I said also that the life of faith and of sacrifice was a life of union with God, and first through purity. It is only by the holy light of purity that the soul can attain unto the vision of God. The more you take of your material existence, casting it like a grain of incense into the divine censer, so that it may rise up before God as a cloud of perfume, the more will the soul reach unto supernatural truth. The first step by which the soul must ascend is purity.

You must also hold converse with God by prayer. Prayer! that incomparable privilege of the soul, by which she may say unto God, " Let there be silence in the celestial spheres ; let their harmonious symphonies be for a moment suspended!"

And God lends His ear to this poor child of humanity, whose voice rises up to Him from the depths of the earth below ; God hears and answers. Prayer is the one great action of life. You must rise by the union and tenderness existing between God and you ; you must be able to say these heavenly and blessed words : " I live, but my life is not my own ; it is not the failing life of my intellect, it is not the wayward life of my heart, the tainted life of my conscience, the withered life of my soul; there is something better living within me, and that is Jesus Christ."

And this is the happiness of the supernatural life; the life which should be in you, a life which consists in self-devotion; and this self-devotion ought to be carried out everywhere, and especially in your own homes.

I spoke to you the other day of a great evil in the present day; I did not exaggerate. You have laid down your sceptre in your own homes, the sceptre of abnegation, of self-devotion, of kindness and of affection. It too often happens that your husbands and your families see nothing in you but capriciousness and intractability; dissatisfied minds, and hearts without stability of feeling. I told you how you neglected your domestic happiness and your own homes—the worldly amongst you—for society; the religiously disposed, for churches and sacristies! How you thus thought to escape from what is, after all, one of your essential duties, that of befriending that soul, that intellect which ought to be the twin-sister of your own; of loving that heart which should be one with your own ; of help-ing that conscience which should fraternize with your own ; claiming with it a meeting in heaven ; for, God does not disunite in eternity what He has united in time.

I went on to say how this mission of devotion to your homes should find its irradiation everywhere ; how it ought to diffuse itself upon those who weep, upon souls who mourn, upon all sorrowing hearts, consoling, encouraging, reanimating them, such is the true mission of the " *valiant woman.*"

"Who shall find the valiant woman ?" Who shall furnish us with the type, the example of the supernatural life ? I wish, my sisters, to show you this example in the Virgin Mary. This will be the conclusion of our retreat.

And I would say a few words to you on this "valiant" and incomparable woman. I have no wish to preach to you a discourse on the Blessed Virgin, such as you often hear, but which passes through your soul as some sort of conventional formulary. In order to bring thoroughly before your minds all that the Blessed Virgin is, and what you may yourselves become by trying to imitate her admirable virtues, something more is necessary than mere sentimental phrases. What then is this valiant woman? How can you reproduce her in your lives?

Oh! may our blessed Mother inspire my tongue; bless these last words which I address to your souls, giving them the fruitfulness of the eternal seed, so that when you leave here you may, like the Mother of God, shower around you charity, light, and every Christian virtue.

When we read in Holy Writ the page of the Old Testament which I have quoted, we are touched to find Solomon pronouncing these words amidst the infirmities of paganism and the degeneration of the Jewish people: "Who shall find the valiant woman?"

He paints a portrait which appears ideal, for it is that of a really Christian woman. He seems as it were to have pre-conceived the "valiant woman," for in his picture he describes Mary. There are three things which constitute the valiant woman: a great idea, a great heart, and a great influence.

Now in Mary we find precisely these three things: a great idea, a great heart, and great influence ; a thought, a feeling, an action. Nor are you, my sisters, made up of aught else ; you are composed but of thoughts, feelings, and actions. Thoughts, often but trivial and light ones, directed perhaps to some personal adornment. Feelings, capricious and mobile according to the various events of life. Actions and influence too often made use of, if not so as to endanger the soul and the conscience, at least at the risk of grievous peril to the well-being of others.

Mary stands out as a prominent figure. From all eternity had God predestined her for her grand mission. God had willed that a woman should be associated in the providential work of redemption. Man, placed in the terrestrial paradise, had fallen ; man, guilty and sinful, degenerated.

When God willed to put on humanity, when He left heaven, when summoning the angels in His train, He descended into this debased valley of creation, well might He then have taken unto Himself a body formed by angelic beings ; and commanded them to mould with their celestial hands the clay of the earth that He might infuse into it a divine life. But He would not ; He took

His place amongst the generations of mankind. He predestined a woman to have the incomparable honour of being His Mother. And just as Almighty God, that Being Who is Himself eternal beauty, that ocean of beauty which hath neither shores nor boundaries, the very plenitude of existence, just as God contemplating the eternal Word, and seeing the splendour of His substance, spoke the ever-living words: " My Son, I have begotten Thee," so Mary, as she reverently gazed at the child lying on the straw in the manger, could say, " My Son, I conceived Thee."

And these two voices from heaven and from Bethlehem combined to give to the world the man-God, the Saviour of humanity, Jesus, the joy of angels, the ever-living friend of the souls of men. Mary then was associated in this great work; she had been prepared by God.

When a painter wishes to depict on his canvas the ideal of his imagination, when he wants to produce a chef-d'œuvre, he sketches features, a face, which seems to him most beautiful; but when he comes to contemplate his work and compare it with his ideal, he sees that it is wanting in harmony, and that he has failed in representing what his mind had conceived. But when God, the Omnipotent Artist, conceives an idea, He is able to represent it exteriorly in all its grandeur. Well, then, God imagined a chef-d'œuvre, and in Mary He created a chef-d'œuvre of grandeur.

And what did He give her? He gave her all beauty, the superhuman beauty of grace. He willed that she should be immaculate in her conception, that her soul should never be tarnished by the faintest breath ; that she should be beautiful in her birth so that her conscience might not be stained by the slightest blemish ; He willed that she should be sublime in her death, glorious in her triumph, queenly in her assumption. And the angels when they saw her ascend, exclaimed : " How beautiful is she who rises like the sun !" It was the Mother of God ! and she was lovely.

Oh ! I understand how saints and doctors have failed in describing her grandeur. I understand that from St. John, who spoke of the Virgin arrayed in her beauty, down to the saints of the Middle Ages, who tried to describe her in the most glowing language, all should have remained powerless. And were even worlds cast down at her feet, they would be as nothing to her, for she has beheld something greater than any worlds ; she has seen God resting in her arms, she has heard Him say words which are above the song of the *suns :* " Thou art My Mother."

It is not therefore wonderful if God has indeed made her sublime ; sublime with a sublimity which is above everything else ; if He has raised her above every other creature, and made her into a chef d'œuvre of creation ! The more she is elevated the less need He abase Himself, and it has been said, that " He did not abhor the Virgin's womb," rather indeed did He make of it a throne of purity and of love ; and these two sweet flowers, purity and love, combined together to form a triumphal arch for Jesus, that He might thus rest in His Mother's womb as in a consecrated tabernacle. So that the Virgin's womb is, after heaven, the only dwelling-place worthy of containing Jesus.

Such then is the greatness of Mary, a greatness adorned with grace and beauty. In her favour did God multiply His marvels. Mary's life was but one perpetual privilege ; there was no discord in her existence. Privileged in her birth, born without taint, she comes into the world without infirmity; privileged in her death, she dies without pain and ascends triumphantly to heaven. Privilege is the law of her existence; doubtless she is the chef d'œuvre of divine power.

And yet although the prophets foretold of her long before; although Moses called her "The woman who was to bruise the serpent's head," and other prophets compared her to the flower of Jesse, to the golden fleece, to the ladder of gold leading up to heaven, still there was to be one more prophecy: herein is . a mystery . . . and this mystery, my sisters, touches you particularly. You have seen this woman created by God, this chef-d'œuvre of the eternal Artist to whom all do honour, you have heard the angels and the prophets singing her praises on their harps of gold. But at last a prophet, an old man advances, he it is who is. to end the prophetic train.   He sees the Virgin ; he looks at her, and drawing near to her he says: "Thou art a mother, and a sword of grief shall pierce thy heart."

This is the finishing stroke of her greatness, the

highest pitch of her elevation. A sword of grief shall pierce thy heart! Thou art the chef-d'œuvre of God, the chef-d'œuvre of the human hierarchy; thou art God's greatest conception. But in order that this chef-d'œuvre be completed, finished, crowned, thou must thyself become a great sorrow. Pass along then through the world, fulfil thy destiny; thy brow shall be encircled by privileges, but thy heart shall be broken; yet from thy glories and thy sufferings mingled together by a divine hand shall there spring forth those bright rays of light which we call love, charity, and virtue.

Yes, my sisters, it is truly a mystery that the only thing which God kept in store for His Mother was the capability of suffering. There exists therein something which disconcerts and astonishes even minds accustomed to fathom the mysteries of the supernatural.

For, never did woman suffer as Mary suffered, and yet I have said how you, my sisters, are pre-eminently destined to suffer; you cannot escape from this law by the pleasures, the distractions of life; if at first you are not overtaken by the tempest of the world, or sorrows of the heart, still, sooner or later will suffering come upon you ; you may put it out of your minds, but its sharp sword will find you out.

The Virgin, the woman, valiant before all others, the Mother of Jesus, had to endure more cruelly, more intensely than any other. Everything in her life was crushed and bruised ; her feelings as a virgin, a mother, a spouse, all her sense of Christian tenderness, if I may so speak, her every feeling, in fact, was crushed and broken like the strings of a harp which gives forth nothing but plaintive sounds.

When she brings her Son into the world, she has not even what every other mother possesses at so blessed a moment of her life ; she is obliged to take refuge in a stable, and to share with the ox and the ass the straw for the manger ; she is forsaken amidst the hardships of winter ; she is in silence and in loneliness, but she bows her head. True, the angels' song will soon be heard ; true, the star will rise over the manger so that rich and poor may know the place, but now her desolation is complete.

Then, when bearing in her arms her newborn babe she comes to the Temple, it is foretold to her by Simeon that this Son who is now her glory, will become to her a sharp sword which shall pierce her inmost soul, that He will be a "sign which shall be contradicted."

After these first maternal trials came those of exile; she is obliged to set out in the middle of the night in order to escape from the storms which threaten her, both from above and below: prosecuting her on account of her Son; the two strongest powers in the world, the power of the populace and the monarchical power, combining together to take away her Child from her.

My sisters, when you are obliged to send your sons to school, how you grieve to part from them, with what tender care do you not surround them. But Mary is poor and desolate, and taking her Child in her arms, she goes into exile without other stay but the old man who is her companion, and he had even for a moment suspected her virtue. Thus does she start on the road for Egypt.

Exile has never been one of your trials, my sisters, it has never been your fate to listen to the sighs of those who are in banishment. Exile! No longer to behold the sky under which we were born, the earth which was our cradle, the grave for which we hoped, the roof which sheltered our childish years, the faces on which our eyes loved to rest; to be deprived of air to breathe! for we find that in other lands the air is no longer the same, that the light is other, that the mountains have not the same outline, neither the sky the same aspect. The poor exile! Not only does he miss these material things, but he has lost the hearts which were dear to him, those hearts which made up the happiness of his life, and his nature requires these affections.

The Mother then bears away her Son into exile! She was compelled, as the holy fathers tell us, to live upon alms; she was obliged to beg her bread, to eat the bread of charity! she, the Mother of the King of the universe, of Him who stretches out the sky like a canopy over our heads! she was obliged to live by her own work, to earn by the sweat of her brow the bread which she gave to her holy Child! Oh! truly was she "the valiant woman!"

At Nazareth she undergoes the anxiety and the pain caused by the absence of her Child, when He remained behind amidst the doctors in the Temple at Jerusalem. Later on, she suffers for several years the pain of separation. True that, for a time, she enjoyed the sweetness of the presence of Jesus Christ. When a mother sees her son return home, even if his face is blackened and soiled by his laborious work, to her he is ever beautiful, for she sees his heart, his soul; Mary is happy when she sees her Son.

But when Jesus enters into public life, when He speaks unto souls, when multitudes live on His words, when He performs miracles both by His hands and by His words, Mary is not there.

When the Jewish women cried out: "Blessed is the womb that bare Thee, and the paps which Thou hast sucked!" Mary was not there.

When upon Mount Thabor, Jesus revealed for a few moments the splendour of His glory; when the Apostles Peter, James, and John, gazing at Him, exclaimed: "It is good for us to be here!" Mary was not there.

When, in presence of His Twelve Apostles, He took bread to make thereof the bread of eternity, and wine which He was to turn into the blood of the life divine; when He said: "Take, eat and drink;

this is My Body, and this is My Blood," Mary was not then there to partake of it.

Mary had endured the maternal suffering of Bethlehem, the sorrows and the trials of exile, the grief when forsaken at Jerusalem ; but now she is to undergo the most terrible of all sorrows, that incomparable sorrow, the agony of sacrifice. Can, indeed, any sacrifice be compared unto hers ?

You speak of your own sufferings, of your grievances, your sorrows. Behold that victim ascending Mount Calvary ! Mary bears the insults of the crowd, their clamours for Jesus' death ; she sees her Son wounded and pierced. That virgin flesh which she bare in her womb, she sees torn in pieces. The face of Jesus is bruised, His body is lacerated and disfigured. And Mary longs to take Him from the cross, to fold Him in her arms, and press Him to her heart ; she cannot. She stands erect, whilst that poor woman who was a sinner, but whom repentance has restored, is bowed down in the agony of her desolation. Mary stands erect ; like the priest at the altar, like the Pontiff of the living God, she takes the victim offered for humanity, her soul consents to the sacrifice. She says, *Fiat!* so be it!

She accomplishes this act of Christian resignation: "Be it done unto me according to Thy word!"

She says it when the Saviour is to be conceived in her womb; she repeats it in order to give to the world the Redeemer, in all the cruel sufferings of His Passion.

Then comes to pass that very miracle of sorrow.

The Son of God begs for a drop of water from humanity: He has given His blood for mankind; it is not granted to Him! the drop of water is refused to Him; nothing is offered Him but the gall of scorn and contempt! He invokes His Father; but He has no longer a Father. He exclaims: "My Father, why hast Thou forsaken Me?"

It is like a cry of despair. And His Mother is there! unable to give Him a drop of water, to tell Him that she has not abandoned Him! Yet more, and this is the culminating point of the sacrifice: the Mother has sacrificed the Son! The Son sacrifices the Mother!

Then the curtain of the Temple is rent in twain;

there remains but for humanity to contemplate this stupendous immolation: a Mother sacrificing her Son, a Son sacrificing His Mother! Thus through a twofold immolation, humanity pure as St. John, restored to grace like Magdalen, may take the Blood of Calvary, the Blood of sacrifice, and steep itself in the tenderness of the Mother, in the divine self-sacrifice of the Son.

Conceive a chef-d'œuvre of beauty. Imagine it great above all greatness, pure above all purity, magnificent above all magnificence. Let the sun be its mantle, the stars its diadem, the world its pedestal—still will it not suffice for the glories of Mary. A very prodigy of suffering: as a woman, a mother, a spouse is she tortured; there is no corner in her heart which is not racked in agony; yet does she stand erect, suffering to the utmost limits of agony.

Mary was a grand conception, a grand idea, a grand embodiment of suffering; hence also springs her wonderful power of influence.

One great thought, one absorbing feeling, gives great power; great suffering gives still greater power, therefore did I say, "Of what is that man capable who has not suffered ?" There is an incomparable power in suffering. The lamentations of sorrow are the strength of the world. Tears are more powerful than the sword or genius ; they are the type, the symbol, the insignia of suffering.

Mary, the chef-d'œuvre of purity and sorrow, is also the impersonification of influence.

Who has the influence of the Virgin ? Since she brought her Son into the world, she brought into it life ; she poured out eternal light upon the world. As some poet has said, all light dates from the cradle of the Lord, consequently from the divine child-bearing of Mary.

She is the protectress of all truth ; since she came into the world every truth of religion has been watched over by her; she is the stem on which every truth rests.

But this is not always understood, although it is part of the divine scheme. I have often met with persons who, on their return to their own Protestant homes, after visiting Catholic cities, said to me : "I saw little pictures hanging up on the walls, little books of devotion, little carved figures ; I saw people bowing their knees before an image; what does it all mean? Are these things signs of idolatry come to life again?"

They do not understand that they are simply external marks of devotion, nothing more.

Nothing stands alone in the world. The Virgin is the guardian of the truth which has been given to man. From the logic of history it is easy to see how those nations which have ignored Mary's power and banished her worship have lost Jesus Christ; and Jesus Christ is truth.

And, indeed, in these days of heresy, the finishing stroke of three centuries of denial of truth has been to look upon divine truth as a simple historical fact. After having denied the sacred prerogatives of the immaculate Mother of the Saviour, the last stroke has been the denial of the divinity of her Son.

Mary protects her Son; she crushes heresy, as she crushed the serpent.

There is great connection between Mary and Christianity. The Virgin Mother is the protectress, the tutelary preserver of truth in the doctrinal order, as well as in the intellectual. But I will not dwell on this idea. Mary is especially the born protectress of charity.

When you behold that Mother sacrificing her Son for the salvation of the world, how courageous ought not you to be, my sisters; how simple ought not self-devotion to appear to you; how easily should you perform the small sacrifices which may be required of you!

Mary is the protectress of self-devotion.

That wonderful hierarchy of religious orders; those women who are but too little known, who are mostly seen through the insults and abuse which are heaped upon them; it is they who are the preservers of Christianity in this our ancient Europe. After the sacrifice of Jesus, after the daily immolation of the sacred victim, this pre-servation is due to those women who have buried themselves in cloisters, in institutions devoted to education, to expiation. Yes, it is due to those silent, devoted women, who, forgetful of themselves, by a perpetual self-immolation, offer themselves to Jesus Christ as a voluntary sacrifice. And God beholds this marvellous hierarchy, flying for shelter to Mary, and following her pure and immaculate banner in order to invoke her to do her honour.

These women are an example of self-abnegation;

how self-devotion flourishes under the auspices of Mary, how popular does it become! If some one of those great men, one of those great minds which might be called the gray dawn of the Gospel, the rationalistic precursors of Jesus Christ; if a man like Plato were to return into our debased and wretched world, were he to return in this century of treachery, of cowardice, and of selfishness, he could not yet fail to be struck by the beauty and the grandeur of the religious hierarchy! He could not but admire the immense amount of self-devotion, the craving for self-sacrifice!

Look at those "Little Sisters," who hide their name, their fortune, beneath a sombre cloak, and, forsaking all things, devote themselves to the poor and to the aged!

Look at those women who shut themselves up in convents, for the sake of bringing up and educating children!

Look at the frequency, the commonness, of such self-devotion among women; which has become a thing of daily occurrence. Oh! it is because Mary watched over the cradle of those young hearts.

And innocence! To keep your innocence, to preserve it amidst the dangers of temptation, amidst the seductions and the trials of your youth, when you felt the approach of the Tempter, oh! did you not then send forth a cry which traversed the universe on its road to Heaven! And Mary came, she protected you, she inspired you with good thoughts, and you rose again, stronger, more hopeful.

Mary, then, is the protectress of innocence.

And what woman has the influence of Mary? After all, she is but a woman. She is not God; she is but the mother of Jesus. We do not elevate her to divinity, we do but call her blessed. She is a child of man, like you, my sisters, but she is a chef-d'œuvre of purity and love, and great is her influence.

For the last nineteen centuries, pontiffs have grown gray in theological battles; doctors and priests have struggled to defend the holy, but often much controverted, orthodoxy of the faith. But all, like St. Jerome, like St. Augustine, have first knelt down and invoked the Virgin Mary, begging her to inspire their words, and to protect the Church and the truth.

Neither were the monks of old wanting in devotion to the Mother of God. Look at the grand figures of St. Benedict, of St. Bernard. They, too, have recourse to Mary, imploring her blessing on their courageous efforts.

See, again, St. Francis of Sales; see Bossuet, laden with years and with renown, kneeling before a poor image of Mary, and begging her to bless his words.

As protectress of truth and of the Church, Mary exercises an incomparable influence, for she is the representative of the supernatural, and this is the strongest influence, the most powerful feeling, which can be brought to bear on the human race.

I end, my sisters, by saying that you, too, in your daily lives, may exercise an immense influence. Upon your grave, as upon your cradle, there will ever be a memento either of good or of evil, of a blessing or a curse. It is your terrible responsibility, but it is also your glory.

You cannot remain neutral here below. Either you will do good, or you will do harm. When you die, you cannot receive a blessing on the right hand, and a curse on the left. Your looks, your countenance, your heart, your movements, your attitude, your whole life, everything belonging to you, is power, an apostolate; everything has an influence. If you would influence for good, you must live in the supernatural, the life divine must live within you. You cannot surpass God. To possess God is the best of all things. To have Him within you is to be full of love, full of generosity; it is the putting-off of your selfishness, of your cowardice, of your day-dreams, of all the meannesses of your life.

Accept your sufferings, therefore, my sisters in Jesus Christ. Love them; ascend even unto the altar of sacrifice, to receive them as from the immediate hand of God, with an uplifted heart, with a courageous soul. Thus to accept the crown of thorns offered to you by God, is the means, not only of sanctifying yourselves, but of being an immense influence for good. If you be the embodiment of but one grand thought, kindled by the fire of noble feelings, and disciplined by suffering, then will you have great influence on those around you. And do you not wish to become influential for good?

I do not know whether, for the last nineteen centuries, there has been in the world's life a more solemn hour than this present one. When the barbarous hordes threw themselves upon the old world in order to destroy it, no doubt it was a solemn moment ; but in those days there were pontiffs, and priests, and Christians, who never rested till these very barbarians became baptized Christians, like St. Clotilde leading Clovis to the feet of St. Remy, by whom this king of a great nation was baptized. Later on, there were fierce combats to save Jesus from Arianism. In the middle ages the fight was for the deliverance of the tomb of Christ. The sixteenth century was the witness of religious controversy ; in the eighteenth, we see the struggle between irony and virtue, between the smile of scorn and beauty of self-devotion. In the nineteenth century, the battle-field is wider, but the fight is reduced to two combatants, God and the devil. Who shall conquer, God or man? Jesus Christ, or the tempter? Shall it be the reign of God, or shall it be the reign of the Evil One? It is an awful moment? Jesus, seeing the conflict, says: " He who is not with Me, is against Me." You cannot escape from this battle. You cannot sit down on a stone by the roadside, and watch the dust of the combat as a mere spectator. You must take your part in it. If not actively, at least by prayer; for prayer is all-powerful, either when it proceeds from the mouth of the young girl, or from that of the desolate widow, or the woman tried by suffering; when the Church is fighting, the weapon of prayer is her best defence. It is the voice which pleads for victory, and obtains it.

Strive then, my sisters in Jesus Christ, and devote your thoughts, your time, your influence, to the service of God and His Church. If, besides this, you make use of the power of expiation; if you learn to pour your sorrows, your sufferings, your tears, not into the trivialities of life, but into the hands of the angels; if you can offer them up as a sacrifice to God; if you will co-operate by your self-devotion, by the careful education of your children, by training their hearts and minds so as to prepare them to become both good and great, you may thus co-operate in the Church's mission; perhaps, even, it may be your privilege some day

to give Her one of your daughters under the virginal veil, or one of your sons to serve Her under
the sacerdotal habit.

Let me speak to you as a bishop. The upper
classes do not generally give their children to the
Church; they are too fond of leaving this honour
to the inhabitants of the country—I am not speaking of this city of Lyons, which is an exception—
but of other large towns of our old Europe. I
have already mentioned this from the pulpit both
in Paris and Vienna. The real misery of the
Church is to see how young men of the upper
classes seem to be incapable of anything better
than driving fours-in-hand, or applauding an
actress. The honour of taking and of holding the
blood of Jesus Christ is not given to them. Whole
generations often pass away before a family gives
one son to the Church.

Christian women! your mother's hearts do not
burn enough with divine love that their exhalations
should bring forth the heart of a priest. Oh! ask
of God that your families may give sons to the
Church; ask of Him that this city of Lyons may
bring forth souls who may immolate and devote

themselves for Him; ask Him that you, in your turn, may have the courage of sacrifice, and that from you, too, may be born an apostle. To speak to men about God, to enlighten the world, to serve Him at the altar; is not this, after all, a grand and magnificent destiny?

Serve, then, the Church, by your words, by your prayers, by your humble and hidden life. Use your influence for all that is good. Suffer courageously. Become imbued with the one great idea of the Supernatural Life, and let this transfiguration shine forth on your countenances, and be felt, like the sunshine, on all around you.

My sisters, let these my last words penetrate into your ears like a voice of thunder. I am going to return to my own city, where the workers for God are not many; help me with your prayers, that when the harvest is ripe I may be allowed to reap it. And since the Head of the Christian Church (who is now on His own Calvary, crowned with His threefold diadem and His crown of thorns,) has placed this cross on my breast, since He has sent me into an arid land to work as in the shadow of death, ask of Him that I may become a saint, that I may, by the means of that influence which attracts souls, propagate in the world those great and holy truths which may lead men to life everlasting.

My sisters, when this nineteenth century, with all its pride and glorious splendour, shall be laid in its tomb, when the twentieth century shall have risen up to laugh at our grandeurs and our childish pretensions; still, over that departed century, will two figures be seen standing forth in broad relief.

First, the figure of Pius IX., that wonderful Pontiff, that countenance shining with angelic beauty, that privileged soul seeing nought but God and the Supernatural Life, giving to the world so marvellous an example of patience, truth, pardon, and saintliness. Side by side with this great Pontiff, you see rising up the austere, emaciated figure of that poor and simple country priest, in whom dwelt the Spirit of God, whom crowds visited in his humble presbytery—the Curé d'Ars.

Pius IX. and the Curé d'Ars will rise up, bright and shining, amidst the darkness of a degenerate century; for there is nothing fruitful save the Spirit of God; He alone is our strength.

My sisters, if you wish to have real influence, you must become endued with the spirit of holiness.

This is my last, as it was my first, advice. Be saints; and you will then become the noblest, the most powerful influence here below; the sweetest, the best helper of God and His Church. You will become the valiant women of the Bible.

R WASHBOURNE, PRINTER, 18 PATERNOSTER ROW, LONDON.

www.ingramcontent.com/pod-product-compliance
Lightning Source LLC
Chambersburg PA
CBHW020922120726
47905CB00008B/2335